CLAIMED BY A DRAGON

Fallen Immortals 9

ALISA WOODS

ISBN-13: 9798869394781

Chapter One

ERELAH'S MATING GOWN LAY IN A PUDDLE ON THE FLOOR.

Leksander's lips were gentle, so gentle. A tiny brush against her bottom lip. A flick of his tongue, just the tip, along the top. His panting huffs of breath were the hardest part of his kiss, buffeting her parted lips, exchanging heated gasps with her.

Every other part of him was *hard*.

His well-muscled arm wrapped around the small of her back holding her standing firmly upright. His other arm hooked under her leg, the crook of his elbow capturing the back of her knee, controlling the exact angle in which he took her. Everywhere the rippling dragon-strong muscles that powered his body, their silky steel giving only slightly under her fingers as she grasped hold of his shoulders, the back of his neck, the broad expanse of his chest. But hardest of all was the thick, heated cock he was driving up into her, again and again.

They were standing in the middle of a dark, damp cave having the hottest sex of her life.

It was all she could do to hold on.

"Erelah," he gasped between thrusts. "Brace yourself."

Her heart fluttered, like the feathers on her wings might if she were using them to fly instead of arching them back, braced against the wall to counter Leksander's grunting, growling, ever-stronger thrusts. They had made love before—and she knew it was Love now and not Lust, not Sin—but that was when she was only angeling, and not the mate of a dragon. Now that he'd sealed her with his mark and implanted her with his child, some of his raw dragon magic had fused with her angel power. The passion she'd felt before seemed to grow stronger with every climax. And Leksander, though she'd brought him back from his wyvern form, seemed to retain some of that animal wildness in their lovemaking. The way he pounded into her with abandon. The way he commanded her into positions she'd never dreamt of. His hard body, soft lips, and growling voice brought her to climax again and again and again.

It was all good for the baby, he told her.

Such perfection seemed more a dream than reality.

Leksander thrust in deep and held while he reached down to lift her other knee from the floor. "Ride me," he commanded, but she could hardly do otherwise. His hands gripped her bottom, and he controlled both her body and his, lifting her and slamming her back down on his cock. He grunted harder with each stroke, and she felt the full length of him as he slid deep, sparking magic wherever they touched. That was on top of the maddening sense of *fullness* she always had with his cock buried inside her. She'd never known another man—Leksander was the first to take her, and he would be the last—but she couldn't imagine physically taking a man any larger than him. Perhaps it was her angeling magic somehow returning her to a virgin state between strokes. It seemed impossible, but each swift impalement felt like that first time when he was determined to have her—and she him—yet she had not been at all confident he would fit.

"So damn tight," Leksander growled through his teeth, speaking her thoughts and thrusting harder into her.

She gasped with the new violence of it, her flesh quivering around the length of him. It was as if he grew more fevered the closer she came to climax... and she was close. So close. An unbearably delicious quivering took hold of her, thrilling from her toes—which flopped madly in the air with each thrust—to her puckered-hard nipples to the core of her sex that he was mercilessly bashing. His raw and feral passion was coaxing her closer and closer, even though he'd already brought her to more orgasms than she could count. They'd only been mated for one night, but it was an endless series of couplings.

The angle at which he was taking her now... she was gasping with each plunge. *"Angels of light."* She clasped her hands around his neck, holding tight while he lifted her body away from his then slammed it back, again and again.

His kisses turned from fleeting touches to harder presses to small nips as he worked his way down her neck. When he reached her shoulder, he sunk his teeth in for a proper bite, the kind that thrilled her and spiked that small bit of pain that crashed her over the top. Then she had no more air for words, just angelsong blasting out, as the orgasm rocked her and rocked her. She vented the power of it so she could stay close to him, feel his own climax rise up and twitch his body, from his bulging arm holding her midair to his pulsing cock buried deep inside.

"Holy fuck," he croaked out, releasing her from his bite, his voice hoarse from all the crying out and cursing and gasping they'd done all night. "So good. So fucking good.

Every, single time. Goddamn, you are hot, angel girl." He was murmuring now, rocking her close, still buried deep, but all violence fleeing with the ebbing of his release. He talked like this to her, sometimes, especially in the throes. So many words, saying so little. Yet they were like a blanket of love that wrapped around her. She lifted her wings free from where they buttressed her against the rocky cavern wall and wrapped them around her beloved.

"Angels are hotter than dragons," she whispered in his ear, shifting where she held him to a more comfortable embrace.

"You got that right," he breathed. He was still inside her and seemed reluctant to leave. Her body hummed, so she was in no hurry, either.

"Angelings who are mated to dragons are hotter still," she noted.

He playfully squeezed her bottom and nipped at her earlobe. "No argument from me."

She meant temperature. He meant the sexy allure of her body. She didn't correct him, just smiled as she nuzzled his cheek.

After a moment, he suddenly pulled back. "Wait, you're not... *too* hot, are you?" The concern etched on his face sent a tremor through her. She was so attuned to him now, a strangeness given how long he had defied her understanding.

She touched his cheek quickly. His skin was always cool to her now. "No, my love. Just the normal blazing inferno."

The baby pulsed inside her, responding to his father's nearness and their passion. Her body hummed with the normal heat of an angeling plus a little extra dragonfire, but even with the heat of their lovemaking, it was normal. *Safe.* Nothing like that searing heat that came before when her angel nature fought with his dragon magic. That fire had nearly consumed her… yet, in a miracle she had no right to expect, she'd endured it and come out the other side.

And now she carried his child.

The joy of this continued to surge up at random times.

Leksander peered at her. "Why the smile?"

"You just gave me another orgasm." She tried to temper the smile, but such joy is not easily contained.

"That's not why." But he was lopsided grinning at her, a look that also made her heart flutter. Her Love for this man was True… but it was also still so new. Like the tiny child inside her, literally made from their love, it was fresh and sparkling and still hit her at odd times. Like when Leksander smiled like this. It struck her how long she had known him and how few smiles had come with those decades.

"No, that's not why." She was pledged to Truth with him, in all things, especially now.

He frowned a little, a shadow falling on his face and quenching the light of his smile. Then he eased out from her body, lifting her clear of him and setting her down on her feet. A delicious ache filled her as her muscles stretched and released, inside and out.

"Is it the baby?" Leksander asked. He was running the back of his hand along her cheek, a motion she'd figured out was his way of checking for the internal magical fire that almost took her life.

"The baby is perfect."

This relaxed his shoulders, and it was the simple truth. As an angeling, she loved all humans, but now she carried a tiny one inside her. It constantly sang to her of the beauty of its soul, pure and innocent and righteous. It was also made of angel and dragon and a flickering of fae from Leksander's lineage through the House of Smoke… but it was the *human* she carried that shone brightest of all. She'd been afraid that the sealing or making the baby would steal her wings—that she would turn shadow or simply lose them altogether—but the only tarnish was a little dust from the rocky cave walls.

Leksander slipped under her outstretched wing, around to her back, and urged her to extend her wings fully. As she did so, he reached from behind to grasp hold of her breasts, kneading her nipples just short of pain—which sent a perverse shock of pleasure to between her legs, even as her sex still pulsed from the orgasm. She now had an unobstructed view of the mouth of the cave… and the morning sun pinking up the sky. The chill breeze of night still washed in, and she welcomed it as it bathed her skin. She lifted her arms, stretching the lovemaking aches, and strained against Leksander's hold on her breasts. He groaned and slipped one hand down to her sex, massaging the flesh there still inflamed by pleasure. It was so sensitive, it almost hurt… and another perverse thrill of pleasure spiked through her. What magic was this? An alchemy of pleasure and love and pain that somehow enhanced all three.

She leaned further into his touch.

"Fuck," Leksander whispered behind her. "You're so sensitive to my touch." He dipped his head to nip at her shoulder and groaned. "I want to take you to your limits, Erelah. I want to find them and break them."

Her flesh tingled all over with those words. "Angels and fae have tried breaking me, dragon prince. None have succeeded." She grinned. She knew he liked this kind of talk.

He groaned and tightened his grip on her breasts. She could feel his cock stiffen and press into her back, already set for more. This response was satisfying to her, and she was tempted to begin again, the slow dance they had performed all night, making their love manifest in the world with their bodies and words and touches. But the new day was upon them, and the world outside the ward-protected cave wouldn't stay silent and dark much longer.

They needed to talk.

She folded her wings and willed them to magically stow in her back such that she appeared fully human.

"Hey," Leksander complained. "Bring those back."

Her wings excited him. Her whole angel nature seemed to add to his pleasure as if his wild wyvern beast took greater pleasure in possessing one of angelkind. Was it that they were immortal enemies, tracing back in time to the beginning? To the very Fall? She had both angel and dragon inside her now, initially warring but now fused in an orgasmic kind of love. She understood the attraction of light to dark, dark to light… and that was why, if they were to talk at all about the serious matters facing them, her wings must be stowed.

It would help if she had clothes as well, so she stepped out of Leksander's hold and conjured them. A simple angel toga would be too revealing—and arouse Leksander too much—so she chose a long-sleeved white blouse and trim dark pants, the kind she'd seen human women wear.

Leksander's face was a study in disappointment. "Well, that's just not fair."

She laughed and came back into his arms, holding his naked body against hers. "I will perform a sexual act of your choosing. *After* we discuss important matters."

His eyes hooded, and he held her tight against his stiff cock. "What kind of sexual act?"

"Of your choosing. As I said."

Interest sparkled in his eyes. "What if I were to conjure… restraints?"

The dragon essence inside her spiked a sudden *need* through her. These games Leksander liked to play were invariably ones she enjoyed. *Immensely.* "Pain and pleasure are more intertwined than I suspected." She ran her tongue along her lips just to see the look of pleasure-tormented pain it caused on Leksander's face. "And you haven't come close to my pain tolerance yet, dragon prince."

Leksander tipped his head back, eyes closed, and whispered, *"Fuck me."* Then he snapped his head forward, eyes blazing. "What do you want to talk about? And how short can we make this conversation?"

She couldn't contain her joy-grin. It was a wonder to her that she'd denied herself these pleasures—not the sexual ones as much as the teasing, the closeness, the sense of unity with this muscular, bright-souled man—as long as she had. They indeed had many years to make up for.

She tried to temper her smile for the seriousness this conversation required. "We must leave the cave at some point. As angeling, I may not need much in the way of sustenance or rest, but this baby is half human. I will require more than normal."

The lust still hooding Leksander's eyes vanished. He slipped his hands to her cheeks. "I am such an idiot. A dragon mate's appetite is legendary. Are you hungry, my love? Thirsty? We've been up all night..." The worry on his face was rapidly escalating into panic, and he was now scanning the walls of the barren cave of his tomb as if he would find a forgotten loaf of bread. He could conjure one, but it would be made of magic, not sustenance.

She pulled his hands from her cheeks and held them. "I am fine for now." She smiled a little. "You are very distracting, dragon prince."

He scowled. "I'm a horrible excuse for a mate."

That flashed anger through her, killing her smile. "I would not mate with a horrible excuse for a man. You are no such thing."

He gave her an exasperated look. "I only meant…" He grasped her hands tighter and pulled her in for a quick kiss. "I'm horribly smitten with you, Erelah. I would give my life for you and the baby in a heartbeat. But you have to understand how my love for you has always been my weakness. And now that I have you…" His voice trailed off, but she didn't need words to know.

"We must do *everything*—all the things—my love." She whispered this now because they'd drawn closer, and she felt the tremble of his heart as if it were her own. "We must love, and make love, and protect our baby. This baby already has enemies. Shadow angels. The fae. There will be many who seek to destroy me and our dragonling, and we must not let them. But we must also *live*. Because I have no idea if I am strong enough to carry this child of yours, not all the way. And I don't want to miss…" She let her urgent need to touch him take over, lifting her fingers to trace his lips. "I want all the things. A lifetime's worth of things. Even if it only lasts a few weeks."

Leksander's face was a torment to see. "The pregnancy is six weeks. After that, we can—"

She stopped his words with her fingers. "There may be no *after*. You know this."

"I can't think…" He swallowed. "I *won't* lose you."

She nodded. "And I will fight to the death anyone who wants to harm our child." She threw a glance at her blade, tarnished and shoved in a corner of the cave. It still was covered with the tar of the demon she slayed while freeing Leksander from its grip. "But I don't even have a decent blade. The wards will protect us from anything immortal, but eventually, we must leave. Return to the keep. It's a better safehold. And I will need a better weapon. It is the transit that will be most risky. We should make a plan to ensure success."

"Of course." Mercifully, the torment was gone from his face, and that cool intellect she prized among his many good traits returned. "I'm just not sure how to accomplish it. The fae have shown they will stop at nothing to stop the treaty from renewing. Normally, the treaty would protect us both—me as a prince of the House of Smoke, you as my mate—but Zephan's managed to threaten my brother's mates before me, so I don't put anything past him. And because you're angel… everything is different."

She nodded, a chill washing through her body. She was uniquely in danger, for many reasons. She snuggled closer into his arms and regretted that she choose to clothe for this discussion. "Shadow angels care not for the treaty. They will strike as they please, kill whom they wish. And my father's rival, Elyon, has a lust for blood and chaos that would be served by my destruction."

Leksander's coolness collapsed into anger. "As far as I'm concerned, the entire angel realm is a threat. Your father is still shadow, and I don't care if Markos is an angel of light. He has his own motives for things."

Erelah blinked and leaned back. "Markos would never hurt an angeling of light."

But Leksander's scowl didn't go away. "He wants us to mate, but not because of the treaty. Or the House of Smoke. Or even because he cares about you. He visited me, gave me a blessing…" He stopped at her surprised look. "Yeah, I know, right? *A blessing.* Because it's fucking important to him that our mating be successful, and he thought that would help. He said it would be a 'new day for angels' if you and I were to mate and you stayed in the light." He slid his hands back to holding her shoulders and peered into her eyes. "I don't give a fuck if you're light or shadow or somewhere in between. You're mine. I love you." He slipped a hand to her belly, which was as flat as it had been the night before, even if the tiny spark of their child burned glory within it. "And this is *our* child. He belongs to the House of Smoke, not Markos's Dominion. I don't *care* what all this means for angelkind. I only care about you. And us. Our family."

His words made her heart swell, and the joy was threatening to break out into a smile once again. "I know," she said simply. "And you're right to be concerned. This baby…" Her hand covered Leksander's at her belly. "The angels will want him, both light and shadow. My own father, a pure angel, couldn't manage to stay in the light through a mating. And he didn't carry the child himself." Emotion welled up in her, the kind of surge that had battered her all night—pleasure, yes, and joy too, but also a terror at losing everything she had suddenly gained. Fear was a stranger to her. Once she feared the Fall, her own personal decadence winning out, but now… now there was so much more at stake. So much more to lose. And she was mere angeling. If her father, a True Angel, couldn't remain in the light… if she were to fall to shadow again during the pregnancy… or the pregnancy itself were to fail… those all seemed too likely.

"Hey," Leksander's voice was soft, and his touch on her cheeks even softer. "It's going to be okay."

But that wasn't Truth, and Erelah wanted only Truth between them. "I may die, Leksander."

"Don't say that." It was causing him pain, and she regretted that.

"I'm not afraid to die myself—"

"*Erelah.*"

"If the choice is me or the child, Leksander, you must save our dragonling."

"*Stop.*" Tears glassed his eyes. He pulled her in for a kiss. And another. "I will make a plan for us to safely return to the keep. I'll do everything to protect you *both.* But please... Erelah... don't speak of your death. I can't bear it."

Her heart ached. For all the danger she was in, it was Leksander who stood the greatest risk. She was no fool; he was *dragon* with enemies both angel and fae, who were much more powerful. It made her heart want to leap from her body and sacrifice itself for him. Yet that was impossible, too. There were literally *weeks* of danger ahead—six to be precise—and already her heart was breaking because of it.

He was holding her face and nuzzling her hair and murmuring his *I love you's* to comfort her. *This man.* Her True Love for him was her armor and her shield. It would carry her through because nothing so righteous could be allowed to perish. A wave of joy returned, bringing a heat riding along on its wings. She had a sudden need to be next to him, skin-to-skin, spilling her burning love out of her chest, showing it through acts and touches and kisses and sweet, sweet heat.

She magicked away her plain clothes, leaving herself bare everywhere.

Leksander's sharp intake of breath spiked heat through her.

Then she unfurled her wings—still snow white—and he exhaled a long, shaky breath. Then he grabbed hold of her, pressing the length of her body to his, and kissed her deeply. His tongue was cool against the immortal heat burning inside her, and its probing of her mouth was both deliciously cool and flushing heat between her legs. His cock had sprung to life again, trapped now between their bodies, but rigid and beckoning. She had promised him sexual acts of his choosing… but first, she longed to have a different part of him in her mouth.

As soon as he broke the kiss, she dropped to her knees. Before he could protest, she had taken the tip of him into her mouth and sucked hard. He gasped satisfactorily, then cursed, then grabbed hold of her hair right at the scalp to guide her. But she'd been taking notes through the night of what pleased him most, so she knew just where to slide her tongue, just how fast to stroke, and how to bring her hand up to help with the thick, deliciously masculine length. She couldn't take him in too far, but the part she could…

He groaned and pulled her head away from her task. "Stand up," he commanded.

The growling restraint in his voice spiked an ache between her legs. She scrambled to her feet, making sure her wings were unfurled to the full extent the cave would allow. He still had hold of her hair.

"You said *any* act I preferred."

"Yes." She was already breathing hard.

Still holding her hair with one hand, Leksander used his other to conjure a flurry of wide black ribbons that flew around her. They lashed her wrists and ankles and chest, but all with a whisper of silky smoothness.

"What is—" Before she could finish, she was yanked off her feet. But she didn't go far. The ribbons pulled *tight*, leaving her spread-eagled in the air. A harness wrapped her chest, framing her breasts with the support of the ribbons, which also trailed a line up to the rocky ceiling where they were anchored with a hook. Her wrists were likewise bound by tethers to the ceiling, her arms pulled wide. Her legs were tied at the ankle, spread wide, the black ribbon securing her to the floor, even as her toes dangled a couple inches above its rocky bumps.

She was exposed, vulnerable to whatever Leksander's intentions. And the lust-filled look on his face said he intended... *much.*

She struggled a little against the restraints to test them. She could easily break free, but not in a million years would she break her promise to Leksander. The twitching brushed her extended wings against the ceiling and brought forth a low growling from Leksander's chest.

"Hold still." He reached out to pinch her nipple. "Or this will take even longer."

Heat was already gushing between her legs. Whatever he intended, she fully wanted him to *start.* But she obediently held still. Truth be told, it reminded her of some Penances her cohort chose, paying for some infraction by immobilization. It cultivated Humility and Patience, Virtues she struggled with as well.

Leksander slowly worked his way behind her, his hand exploring every crevice of her body along the way. Then she felt his hands and mouth on her wings, trailing his fingers through her feathers, nipping kisses on the blood ones—the ones that carried sensation and that he seemed particularly fond of. She struggled for stillness, his touch maddeningly heating her up while also being slightly ticklish. He crossed her back with feather-light kisses then attended, even slower it seemed to her, to the other wing. By the time he slid around to her front, she was trembling with need. She bit her lip to keep from crying out for him to *touch her...* for real, and with the expert pleasuring he was capable of. Instead, he continued to torment her with light touches and flicks of his tongue all over her breasts, her belly, her arms, and then legs. When he was feasting on her toes, she nearly cried out with the aching tremor running through her.

She kept it in but only through gritted teeth.

She was certain he had touched every single inch of her body… save one.

Finally, he kneeled before her, leading with his artful tongue and plunging it into her sex. Then she *did* cry out—with relief as much as anything. As he moved with the sure skill he had in pleasuring her, she couldn't help the whimpers that escaped her mouth. They only seemed to spur him on, the flicking of his tongue becoming more rapid, his fingers joining in the torment. Just as she felt the power of her climax gathering, the quivering of her flesh starting… *he stopped.* Moving away from her sex entirely, he slid his hands behind her and up to her wings, teasing the sensitive feathers once more.

He was nearly face-to-face with her, a wicked grin on his face as his hard body pressed against her breasts and belly. His cock speared into her just above her sex, inches too far to bring her the pleasure she was dying for.

"What do you want, angel girl?" His smile was pure lascivious pleasure.

"*Release,*" she breathed.

"I'm not going to release you," he said, eyeing the ribbons, although that wasn't what she meant. And he knew it. He trailed his hands through her feathers. "Not yet."

"Please," she begged. He knew what she wanted. And she understood this game, or at least, she saw the way he was playing it. But that didn't stop the need from leaking into her voice.

He chuckled. "Oh, I like it when you beg." Then he brought his hands forward and lavished attention on her breasts, sucking and licking and pinching until she felt a quivering rush of an orgasm building simply from that. Just as she was getting close, he stepped away from her body. His gaze danced over her form, grin wicked on his face.

She growled in frustration. "You would make an excellent Master of Penance," she complained.

His eyes flashed. "Oh, we'll definitely talk more about *that* later." Then he knelt in front of her again, and she cried out even before his tongue hit her inflamed and sensitive nub. She rushed at her climax, and once again, he stopped—this time, just pulling away momentarily, then returning for more. Again and again, the torment continued until she was simply babbling, begging, crying out for him to *finish*.

When he pulled away and stood, she thought she might not endure it. She might have to break the restraints—they were tissue and magic, hardly holding her against her squirming. Then she would blast him across the cave and have her way with him. Even as that fantasy spooled out in her mind, he magicked her restraints to *move*. Just a small movement, though, just enough to lower her toes to the floor and allow her to stand, legs still spread, arms and wings still raised.

Then he pressed his body against hers, the thick length of his cock like a rod of steel between them. His breathing was as labored as hers. He threaded his fingers into her hair and fisted his hand there. His other hand slipped behind her, grabbing hold of her shoulder and pulling her down slightly, keeping the restraints taut. He dipped down to position his cock at her entrance. She nearly cried out for joy, but then she imagined him taking her, thrusting into her, only to *stop* once again.

His lips trembled against her breast. "All the things, Erelah. All of it. All the time." His words were heated whispers that made her sex quiver even harder.

Then he thrust up into her. *She screamed.* The sudden fullness and the satiation of *need* were too much. His grunt bounced off the walls, then he thrust again and again. Each time, she cried out, joy mixed with heat tossed with need. A swell of tension filled her, lighting up every nerve in her body, rushing her toward her peak. Just when she was sure he would stop again, he growled a deep and guttural sound and kept thrusting, bringing her blessedly over the top.

Her body *exploded* with pleasure.

It wracked her, trembling and thrashing and bucking with it, pulling at her restraints in jerks and twitches, her angelsong crashing out onto the walls. Leksander's cry as he came was likewise wild and ragged, his thrusts even more unleashed. She came and came, and it seemed like it would just go on forever, but eventually, the pulses of pleasure slowed. Each one, each small aftershock, was still an earthquake, but just a tremor of pleasure, not an earth-shattering one.

She could hardly catch her breath.

Leksander held her, still buried, but his forehead was bowed, fallen forward against her chest. His heavy pants coated her skin.

"That might..." he breathed. "That could actually kill me."

Erelah was limp in her harness. She had no words to share.

Leksander looked up with worry. "Are you all right, my love?"

She had to lick her lips to respond—they'd grown parched. "You can do *that* any time you wish. No need to ask first."

The smile grew slowly on his face, but it kept growing until she thought it might break.

Then a voice sounded behind Leksander. "Well, this is interesting."

She and Leksander both jolted. Leksander whipped his head around to look, but Erelah had already seen him —*Leonidas*. Leksander's brother and a prince of the House of Smoke. He stood perched at the mouth of the cave, the toes of his boots barely holding him to the ledge just outside the wards. His eyebrows were arched, taking in the full measure of her naked body, strung up and splayed out. If she weren't so sated with pleasure, she might be embarrassed.

"Can't say I pegged you for this," Leonidas said to his brother with a smirk. "But I approve."

Leksander growled and conjured a curtain of privacy between them.

But the moment had come.

Time for them to leave.

Chapter Two

"I don't like this." Leksander stood just inside the wards protecting the cave.

"We'll be fast." Leonidas glowered at him, barely keeping balance on the lip outside.

"Four dragons. Four packages," his brother Lucian said, likewise clinging by the edge of his boots to the rocky ledge next to Leonidas. "Enough to last you a week. Maybe two. In and out in under thirty seconds."

"More than enough time for a shadow angel to pop up," Leksander replied, arms folded. Angels and angelings —hell, the fae for that matter—traveled by inter-dimensional doorways. And they went wherever they damn well pleased, invading each other's Dominions at will. That was a death sentence, but still. Leksander didn't like the idea of lowering the wards protecting the cave… even for thirty seconds.

Lucian sighed. "We'll time it just right, and we've got a dozen dragons on guard. Any angels will have to plow through those first. By then you can get the wards back up.

And it could be faster than thirty seconds. Maybe half that." They'd been working out the logistics all morning, and the sun was blazing high in the sky.

It was the right solution for right now—deliver some supplies, mainly food and water, then work out a larger plan to move Erelah and the baby to the keep. But when it came down to actually executing, Leksander was struggling to bring himself to do it. To take the risk. *The first of many.* He knew every step of this would be risky, but that didn't mean he had to like it.

"Why are we waiting?" Erelah asked, coming up behind him. They were both fully dressed in conjured clothes—her in an angel toga, but a more warrior kind, less revealing, and him in some simple jeans and t-shirt. If he had to fight, he would shift anyway.

"Thirty seconds," he said. They really hadn't gotten it any shorter, no matter how much he bargained or how much they practiced. "It's enough time for almost anything to happen." What he wanted was to already have Erelah back at the keep, naked, and in his arms. And given she could move through inter-dimensional doorways just as well as the rest of angelkind, it wasn't like they would have to fly back. Most of the time would be in raising and lowering wards. Not a lot of time, but some. Just like shuffling in some supplies to their cave, which was uncomfortable and dusty—it was meant for death, not a six-week stay while growing a dragonling.

She held up her tarnished angel blade. It still glistened black from the demon essence she had drawn into it, almost like the blade had been broken by it. That same demon—the one Erelah drew out of him and into herself —had nearly broken *her.*

"Once you lower the wards," she said, "Markos may

hear my blade calling. But if he comes, I have need of a new blade anyway."

"I don't want him near you." She was fearless, and he loved her for it, but he trusted none of the angelkind right now. Especially the angel who thought Erelah belonged to *his Dominion.*

She scowled. "He's unlikely to respond quickly. Angels take their time and act with measure and wisdom."

Oh, for fuck's sake. But Leksander bit his lip. There was no point arguing about the Virtues of an angel, least of all with an angeling who looked up to him like a father. Given her own father was in shadow, he could understand that. Maybe.

"It's fine with me if he takes his time," Leksander said, keeping most of the bitterness of out his voice. "Besides, the last thing I want is you in a position where you have to use your blade. That's just… I don't want you that close to danger."

Erelah nodded. "Every precaution must be taken for the baby. But my blade may be its last defense."

A chill washed through Leksander—he could too easily see that being true.

When he hesitated, she added, more softly. "I've begun to feel the pangs of hunger, Leksander. The baby needs sustenance."

Leksander sighed and unlocked his arms. What else could he do? "Fine." He turned to his brother's expectant looks. "Thirty seconds. Make it fifteen, okay?"

Lucian nodded and leaped backward off the ledge, shifting midair to his golden dragon form to go coordinate with the others.

"It's going to work," Leonidas assured him. But his brother hadn't been to the shadow world. He hadn't seen the things Leksander had. The hurricane of magic that angels of light and shadow created when fighting. The bloodthirstiness of the shadow world altogether. And that wasn't even counting the fae, who were tangled up in this somehow.

"When the wards are down," Leksander said to his brother. "I'm going to toss out Erelah's blade. I want you to retrieve it and see what can be done to get it fixed. Then bring it back to the keep. I want a plan to move us in the works as soon as possible, and I want Erelah to have a functional blade when it happens."

"You got it." Leonidas turned to Erelah. "There's not a dragon here who wouldn't sacrifice themselves for you, princess of the House of Smoke," he said with a small smile. "And there are a couple of dragon mates back home rooting for you as well."

Erelah seemed uncertain what to say.

Leksander took her hand and squeezed it. "Stop freaking out my mate," he growled to Leonidas, who just chuckled and pushed off the ledge, shifting into his bronze dragon form. He flew away from the edge to join the others gathering on a nearby cliff with the resupply packages.

"I am not freaked out," Erelah said softly. "I am… grateful."

He turned to her. "You are sexy as hell, and I want nothing more than to have you in my bed back at the keep." He pulled her close and kissed her, mostly to cover up the fact *he* was freaked out by the idea of lowering the wards. He'd tried to think of a way to make interlocking wards—a second barrier that would lock Erelah safely away while they made this transfer of food and water—but he would have to be *outside* the second barrier to lower the first. That would leave him exposed. And if he died then, she would be locked in. There was no good solution other than simply dropping the wards and hoping his brothers didn't fuck up.

"You are worried," Erelah said plainly, "but this is a good plan. A necessary plan. Then we can move forward."

"You're right." He held his hand up. "Give me the knife. I'll toss it out right before I raise the wards again." She handed it over. "And I want you as far to the back of the cave as possible." The cave was small, and there wasn't really anywhere to go. "I'll conjure a wall that looks like the back of the cave to conceal you. It won't stop an angel or fae who's determined to get in, but it might slow them down. Or at least confuse them." It was the best he could come up with.

She nodded. "They can easily transport past it. And any immortal should be able to sense my presence if they know what to seek. But it might confuse them. A little." She was being kind about his mostly-useless gesture.

He pulled her in for another kiss. "If someone gets past me and this fucked up angel blade of yours, I expect you to kill the hell out of them. No matter who they are."

"I will protect our baby." And *that* he knew to be an unquestionable truth.

"Okay, go." He would lose his nerve if he drew this out much further.

She strode to the furthest corner of the cave, and he quickly conjured a wall that looked very cave-like to conceal her. Then he turned to face the mouth of the cave. A full squad of dragon warriors was circling in the air above the canyon his tomb was carved from. Four of them carried bulky wooden crates in their talons. A half-dozen others circled those, forming a protective guard. Lucian was among them, serving as the lead. Leonidas was closer to the tomb, his bronze scales catching the brilliant shine of the sun as he hovered and swooped, crisscrossing a pattern that blocked entry to the cave. Another half dozen dragons were doing the same, a constantly rotating phalanx of guards to literally, physically block the cave with their talons and teeth and dragonfire.

An angel would blast through them like tissue paper.

Leksander took a steadying breath, lifted his hand to give the ready signal, then shifted to his dragon form. According to the plan, that was the visual cue to start the run. Lucian screeched to his four crate-carrying dragons, leading them forward, picking up speed as they headed for the cave. Leksander clutched Erelah's damaged blade in one set of talons while he waved the other across the mouth of the cave, bringing down the wards. The instant they were down, he reached out mentally to his brothers.

Now! he telepathically commanded to Leonidas.

Lucian and his dragons had nearly reached the rocky wall face that his tomb was carved in. Leonidas banked hard away from the cave, and he and the other dragons held their guard stations in the air, hovering while Lucian's dragons, one-by-one, swung the crates into the cave then banked up hard to avoid crashing into the mountain. The crates tumbled across the rocky floor and banged against the false wall Leksander had erected. As the fourth one sailed through, Leksander tossed Erelah's blade out into the bright morning air, then lifted his taloned hand to conjure the wards once again.

A split-second before he finished, Tajael appeared in the cave.

It was too late to stop. The ward was up. The cave was sealed.

Tajael was inside.

Leksander roared, blasting dragonfire at the angeling. The rolling blue fire buffeted the crates, catching one on fire, but the angeling somersaulted over the spray and shot feet first toward Leksander, knocking him clear across the cave and against his own wards. The magic of the barrier sparked and seared heat across his back, but he bounced off and landed on his feet. Leksander charged, leading with all four taloned hands and feet. He caught the angeling in the chest, sinking his claws and drawing blood, but Tajael just grabbed hold of his scaly arms and whipped him around, sending him crashing so hard into the rocky wall of the cave, he broke a chunk of it loose.

"Dragon prince!" Tajael shouted. "Stay down."

Fuck that. Leksander heaved his head up, spraying dragonfire as he got his feet under him. Tajael magically twisted out of the plume, disappearing from one end of the cave and reappearing at Leksander's back. The angeling shoved him to the ground, this time forcing Leksander's face against the dusty floor and holding him with what felt like the force of a rockslide.

"Leksander!" Erelah's voice rang out. *Close.* Too close. Leksander twisted his face away from the dirt.

She had magicked her way out from behind the rockwall camouflage.

"Erelah!" Goddammit, what was she doing?

Tajael instantly released him. Leksander rolled, trying desperately to grab the angeling's wings or toga or legs—anything to keep him from reaching Erelah—but Tajael was too fast. Leksander roared his panic and frustration and heaved himself up from the ground only to find...

Tajael flat on the ground at Erelah's feet.

Leksander stumbled to a stop, cutting short his raging charge. Erelah looked down at the angeling with a horrified expression, but it wasn't fear on her face. And she wasn't holding Tajael down or threatening him. The angeling had simply prostrated himself before her, kneeling forward until he was folded in half, face down in the dirt, arms spread wide.

"Get up!" Erelah gasped out.

"Tell your mate," Tajael said, not moving a muscle. "Tell him I would never harm you."

"Do not prostrate before me!" Erelah's eyes were wide and panicky. She bent down and grasped hold of Tajael's toga, yanking up. The angeling was dead weight, refusing to move.

"Tell him," Tajael said, head still bent.

She dropped him and stepped back, the same look of horror still plastered on her face. She dragged her gaze up to meet Leksander's. "Tajael will not hurt me." Then she looked down again at the angeling. "He has pledged to serve me."

Leksander's blood was boiling—the adrenaline still surging from the brief and panicky fight—and he had no idea what this pledging business meant, but it appeared that Tajael would not harm Erelah. Or try to steal her away. Although, technically, the angeling had nowhere to go. He was locked in the cave with them.

"Get up!" Erelah demanded again, and this time Tajael did.

His snow white toga was a horror show of red from where Leksander's talons had sliced through and drawn blood.

"You are injured!" Erelah said this like she blamed Tajael for his own wounds, which calmed Leksander's immediate fears about that.

Tajael bowed his head. "Your mate is very protective. I tried not to damage him." He peered sideways at Leksander. "I trust you are well, dragon prince?"

And other than the anger and humiliation of being

ground into cave dirt... "I have one too many angelings in my cave, but other than that, I'm fucking fine."

"I am relieved to hear that." And he seemed to mean it. "I wish no harm to you, and of course, none to Erelah."

A pulse of magic boomed from the wards, making Leksader jolt and dragging his attention outside. A bronze dragon had just crashed into the ward shield. *Leonidas.* His brother reeled back then leaped for the lip of the cave again, this time shifting human just as he arrived.

Leonidas barely clung to the edge. "Leksander! What the fuck is this?" Dragons were swarming behind him, including Lucian's golden dragon, shrieking and looking panicked. Leksander couldn't hear their telepathy through the wards, only the stiff wind of their wings beating the air and the ordinary sound waves of their screeching.

"It's okay," Leksander rushed out, but he really had no idea what was going on. He turned to the angeling invader. "What the hell, Tajael?" Leksander had been prepared to fight *anyone* who broached the cave—why would Tajael come blazing in if he meant no harm? What did he expect would happen?

The angeling gave a helpless shrug. "I've been waiting for Erelah's blade to sing, but there's been nothing. I feared the worst when I returned from the demon uprising in Seattle to find the House of Smoke in chaos. No one would answer my entreaties from the weigh station. None would confess where the dragon prince had gone. Or his beloved. It was all secrets and lies and…" He turned to Erelah. "I feared for you, but I knew you must be in hiding. If you weren't dead, then you were well hid. And must have a reason for hiding. And if so…" He glanced at Leksander. "If you are mated…" He turned back to her and broke into a smile. "But I *sense* it. The child you carry, Erelah! What a wonder."

"It is," Erelah said carefully. And Leksander was glad to hear the caution in her voice. "But I will protect this child with my life, Tajael." There was a warning in her voice.

Leksander expected Tajael to protest or be confused, but instead, he just nodded solemnly. "As will I." He grimaced and turned to face Leksander. "My apologies, prince of the House of Smoke. I didn't mean to appear threatening. But I suspected you and Erelah may have mated. That you may have created a child, just as you have. And I figured if that were true…" He looked back to Erelah for help.

Understanding dawned on her face. "You wanted to get here first."

Tajael nodded. "You are right to be concerned. This… this *child*… it changes everything." He was staring at Erelah's belly as if he could see straight into her womb. And Leksander supposed he could. Erelah had often spoken of seeing—or really *sensing*—the souls of the humans she rescued from demons. And more than once, Leksander felt as if she were peering directly into *his* soul… as if she could really *see* it.

Erelah frowned. "Have you told Markos what you suspected?"

"No." Tajael was emphatic about that, and somehow, that made Leksander's shoulders relax. Leonidas was scowling from outside the wards, but he gave Leksander a nod. This was good news. "Not that the knowledge of your child will be kept from Markos for long," Tajael warned. "And when he discovers the truth…" He grimaced. "Erelah, I am joyful for you and the child and the renewal of the treaty. But you have to know the consequences of this are… they're almost beyond reckoning for the angel realm."

"You think he would try it," Erelah said, her face drawn down. "Markos has ambition to try it."

"His weakness has always been Humility," Tajael said.

"Try what?" Leksander asked, suddenly lost in this conversation.

Tajael flicked a look to him. "Markos sees the shadow realm grow stronger, century by century, building their armies with the fallen. With angelings created from their Lust."

"Wait..." Leksander said. "Are you saying Markos wants to build an army of angelings too? Like Razael?" Erelah's father had tried to create her without falling into shadow—and failed.

"Markos has *already* been doing it." Tajael gave Erelah a knowing look. "Although by stealing the angelings created by shadow rather than creating his own."

She frowned, but she didn't disagree. "All this time... I believed we were fighting for the light. For righteousness, Tajael."

"And we *are*," he replied, earnestly gesturing to her belly. "But don't you see? If Markos believes he can make angelings without Falling—without going to shadow—then he will. He will attempt it, and others as well. This hope that you offer, Erelah..."

Her eyes were wide. "But they will not be able to do it! It is... complicated. And they would have need of True Love. And... and... it may not even be possible for *me.*"

"I *know*," Tajael cried out. "But Markos will be certain that if a lowly angeling can accomplish it, then surely he can. And if Markos and the other angels try, based only on that hope, they may well Fall."

"And if the True Angels start to Fall..." The horror was even more plain on Erelah's face.

Leksander couldn't be more confused. "So they go to

shadow. So what?" He had to be missing something here. The shadow realm seemed cruel, but it wasn't like they were dead.

Tajael's face grew as serious as Leksander had ever seen. "There are few forces for light and goodness in this world and much chaos, dragon prince. You know this. Your House is key to keeping some of it in balance."

Leksander frowned. "You mean the fae."

"Exactly right," Tajael said. "But your treaty binds the fae only in a very specific way. They may not kill humans who might mate with the House of Smoke. Or heirs of the House of Smoke itself. But there is much other mayhem they can evoke. Just look at what is happening in Seattle right now with this demon uprising!"

Leksander scowled. "I haven't exactly had time to watch the news."

"It is dire and getting worse," Tajael said. "The immortal and mortal worlds are clashing at unprecedented levels, the likes of which hasn't been seen since…" He swallowed. "Well, since humanity actually *believed* in magic. These past millennia of calm between the realms have been kept by one thing and one thing only."

"Angels of the light." Erelah's whisper was both a curse and an answer. She looked stricken, one hand on her belly, the other gazing past Leksander's shoulder, out into the still-churning cloud of dragon wings. "My baby could bring the end of times."

"What?" Leksander's alarm shot up ten levels. "Our baby is doing no such thing." He gently took Erelah's shoulders in his hands and peered into her eyes to catch her attention. "Erelah, my love. Our child is going to save the treaty. He's going to renew it for another five hundred years. He will keep humanity safe." He knew that was

playing dirty, but it also was true—and saving humanity was what every angeling lived for.

She dully nodded, but he could tell she was still turning this crazy idea over in her mind.

Leksander released her and stormed over to Tajael. "Time for you to leave."

Tajael nodded. "I'll keep close. I'll work with your House to guard your retreat. I've pledged myself to Erelah's Dominion."

"Erelah's *Dominion?*" What the hell was the angeling talking about?

But Tajael just went on. "My life is hers, and the baby's, and yours, prince of the House of Smoke. Trust that I will do everything in my power to keep you safe." He threw a concerned look to Erelah, who was now staring at the floor. Then Tajael turned to face the mouth of the cave.

Leonidas was still fuming just outside, watching and waiting for Leksander's next move.

"I'm going to lower the wards for half a second," Leksander said loud enough for everyone to hear. To Tajael, he said, "Make sure you're out before they go back up."

Tajael gave a curt nod. And sure enough, when Leksander lowered and raised them again—as fast as he could gesture the magic—Tajael had disappeared from the cave and reappeared, floating on white wings, in the air outside, next to Leonidas. His brother scowled at the angeling, but he shifted and leaped off the cliff. Tajael followed, returning to the scrum of dragon forces in the air above them.

Leksander turned away from them and went to his mate, gathering her in his arms. She buried her face in his chest. He had no words for her, so he simply conjured a draping of white cloth across the mouth of the cave, sealing off the world from their sight.

He didn't understand half of what just happened, but they weren't going anywhere. He would wait until she was ready to explain.

His brothers and Tajael would have to figure out their next move.

Chapter Three

Leksander had conjured a bed for her.

Before, the roughness of the walls and the floor didn't inhibit the gritty urgency of their lovemaking. He took her standing, from the front and behind, kneeling as well, and even suspended in the air that one time when the soft ribbons of his love bound her. But now, after they had eaten and drunk their fill from the crates, after they'd washed and refreshed with the towels and wipes from their small mountain of supplies, Leksander had made her a bed with white satin sheets and gauzy netting and thick wooden posts at every corner.

As if *now* she needed comfort.

He was right.

"Are you sure you don't want one of these chocolate croissants?" Leksander was busy stacking and organizing the supplies. He'd just cleaned up from their meal.

She was curled on the bed, arms wrapped around her knees, wings hidden magically inside her back. "I think I've eaten enough for the entire pregnancy." And she had—cheeses and bread and fruit, plus pastries and chocolate and some delicate shaved ham. Her angel nature lived off magic, and her human side was buoyed by that. She was half human, but she required far less than half the normal amount of food and rest.

Leksander just nodded and continued his organizing.

Erelah stared at her toes, quietly digging into the fine white satin that covered their bed.

Her heart had turned inside out. What if Tajael was right? What if the birth of her child meant every True Angel with a weakness in Pride would want to build an army of angelings... not by rescuing the fallen's offspring, bringing them back to the light, but by creating *new* angelings themselves? By mating with humans? Angelings of the light, too—they might dare to mate with the humans they were supposed to protect, just as she had. Surely many would Fall. But what if some succeeded? Would they all keep trying? Would it spiral out of control and usher in the End? None knew God's plans, but the End had clearly been spoken of throughout time, by angelkind and humankind both, even from the beginning —from the very first Fall. And it was a simple logic. Every Beginning must have an End.

But how cursed were those who brought it?

A shudder went through her with that thought. She searched inside for the joy that had beamed so effortlessly from her before—when she first knew their love had created this child within her. Now, her chest literally hurt with the heartache that somehow their child might not save the world but bring horrors to it. The child itself, of course, was pure of heart, innocent of all things—it was the world which would go mad when he was born.

"Hey," Leksander said softly, appearing at the side of the bed.

She hadn't even heard his approach.

"Did the food help?" The tension on his face pulled at her heart, too. It felt fragile as if even that small tug might shatter it.

"It has eased my hunger." But she knew he meant the dark mood that had taken hold of her.

He frowned. "Well, that's something, I guess." He eased onto the bed with her, climbing around to stretch his body out, full length, then snuggling his head under her arm. His focus was on her belly, a hand resting on the tight wrappings of her training toga, his lips stealing a light kiss on top. "All right, baby dragon. You got your food. Now let your mama rest."

Her smile didn't quite make it out to her lips, but she felt it inside. She trailed her fingers through his hair. Only a few days ago, it would have been a wonder to touch him like this, much less all the other ways he had touched her. She'd crossed over into another world, and at the same time, it had narrowed to this one tiny cave, her and her beloved. Their child. And the fate of the world.

Leksander leaned back and propped up to sitting next to her. His hand drifted up from her belly and played with the fastenings on her toga, just above her breast. It was held on primarily by magic, but a couple knots also bound it in place. "I might have to figure out how this comes off."

"You created it," she said, dully. "You can magic it away."

"Yeah?" He slid his gaze from her breast up to her eyes, but the interest there died when her expression said *not interested.*

She frowned. This lack of interest bothered her. As if everything good and bright had been extinguished by her fears, even sapping away this brimming heat she seemed to always have with him.

"It's what Tajael said, isn't it?" Leksander moved his

hand back to her belly. "About the True Angels Falling and creating havoc."

She bit her lip and nodded.

"You know that's not your fault, right?" There was a little more fire in his eyes now. He'd been carefully tiptoeing around the cave, allowing her the sour mood that had gripped her, but now it seemed he wished a fight.

But she had no fight in her. "It matters not. What matters is the harm that will come of it. A harm I am powerless to prevent. And yet I'm the cause." The grief of that welled up a literal blackness in her soul. Even when she was fighting the demon she'd called out of Leksander's body, she'd never felt this true darkness. It was one reason she had stowed her wings. She didn't want to see if they had returned to shadow.

Although maybe that was the answer.

As that idea sparked a morbid fascination in her mind, Leksander was moving on the bed to more fully face her. *"You* are not the cause of anything." He was almost angry, but it didn't stir her heart, not the way this idea of returning to shadow did. "What these fucking angels decide to do," he continued, "is completely on *them*. All right? You are doing something… *amazing.* You believed in me. You *loved* me. You took a leap of faith that our love was even possible when no one in their right mind would have thought so."

"You believed," she pointed out. "It was your belief—your *goodness*—that made it possible."

He gave her a crooked look. "You mean my stubbornness."

"That as well." The need to smile tugged at her heart, but it wasn't strong enough to lift it.

Yet he smiled for her and went back to toying with the shoulder knot on her toga. "You know, I really had no idea whether you could love me. All I knew was that I was obsessed. Every night, you were part of my dreams. *My fantasies.*" He gave her a wicked smile and loosened the knot that held her toga firm to her breast.

"So, you were taken with Lust." She could understand it now—the feeling of sexual attraction was bound up with her love for him, but had he Lusted for her before he loved her? That didn't even make sense to her.

"I was *so* taken with Lust." He rumbled that growling sound he often made in the throes of their lovemaking and slipped a hand under her loosened toga to cup her breast.

He teased her nipple with his fingers, but it felt... *wrong.* She moved away from his touch, and he immediately drew his hand back.

"Erelah, my love." He seemed pained, like her heart.

Her shoulders dropped. "I feel a great darkness inside. My love for you is still True, Leksander, but I cannot even picture the act of love right now. Have I broken it? This desire I had for you before... it seems broken."

He seemed to be holding back a smile, which annoyed her. But then he sat up, folded his legs, and scooped her bottom off the bed and into his lap. "You are not broken, my love." He held her cheek and gently kissed her forehead. "You're merely sad. It will pass."

"It doesn't feel like it is passing," she complained.

"Then we shall have to make it pass." He lowered his kiss to her cheek.

"But that is the broken part," she insisted. Then she gestured to the white linen curtain he had conjured across the mouth of the cave to give them privacy. It fluttered lightly in the breeze coming in from outside, and she could hear the screeches and rustlings of the dragons out there. "Tajael is right now working on safeguarding our transit back to the keep. He's pledged his life to protect the baby and me. But what if everything he says comes true? How can I have joy now, if that is where the future leads? How can I make love as if the world isn't in danger because of it?"

Leksander let her vent, and it felt good to get the words out of where they bashed around in her chest. But the look blazing in his eyes said he didn't agree, not in the slightest.

"First of all, forget the outside world." Leksander waved his hand and conjured a rock wall much like the one he used to "hide" her when the wards were down. "This is our mating time, and the world is not invited."

She took a fresh look at the wall—the whisper of wind and distant call of dragons was muted, blocked by the magic and rock of the wall. The silence felt like a cocoon as if they were truly insulated from the world now. It was just her, Leksander, and the baby.

"Second of all," Leksander continued, brushing his thumb along her cheek, "you have only one mission for the next six weeks. To grow a dragonling. Forget the treaty and the world… this is *my child*, Erelah. It is literally my life you hold within you."

In all the drama, she *had* forgotten that part—that Leksander's magic would only renew, his life extending for another five hundred years, if he successfully spawned a dragonling. It was how all dragons worked, but the House of Smoke was most cursed of all, requiring a mate in True Love with them.

Her love would literally save his life.

A spark of joy returned to the darkness inside her. "I wish for you to live, dragon prince." She gave him an earnest look.

"As do I," he said with a smirk. "Not least because I've got decades of fantasies I've yet to play out with you, angel girl."

The joy inside her grew.

He gently kissed her forehead again. Then he pulled back and said in a stern voice, "Lie down, face on the bed."

Her smile finally broke out. "Is this one of your fantasies?"

"No," he said firmly, although there was a glimmer of mischief in his eye. "But you need to relax and put all these thoughts out of your head. I'm going to give you a massage."

"A massage?" She frowned. What kind of thing was this?

"It's where I rub your body all up and down." His brow scrunched up like he wasn't sure if he was explaining it right. "It's to relax your muscles."

"But this is not a fantasy? Not a sexual thing?" She truly didn't understand how this was supposed to work.

"Well, it is, but… no, that's not why I'm doing it." He seemed resolute about this, so she didn't argue. She climbed out of his lap and lay face down on the bed.

He moved on top of her, straddling her legs, his hands hovering over her bottom.

She lifted her head to peer back at him. "Are you certain this isn't a kind of sex?"

He growled and leaned forward, pressing his hands into her shoulders and forcing her flat again. "Yes, I'm certain." But there was a scowl in his voice.

Then he moved his hands over her back, pressing in with his fingers in a rhythmic motion. Her back seemed to rebel at the onslaught, bunching up her shoulders and twitching as he touched her. Her toga moved across her skin, loose from the knot he'd undone in front, so it heated her skin with a kind of friction.

"Relax, angel girl," Leksander whispered into her ear, but his voice was laced with frustration.

If this was supposed to relax her, it was doing a terrible job. In fact, it seemed to have the opposite effect. But she tolerated it as a Penance—Leksander was trying to comfort her, and that she appreciated, but it was more like a very still form of wrestling. Her body fought every movement Leksander's hands wanted to coax out of it.

He leaned back, still perched on the backs of her legs, and sighed. "The toga's getting in the way," he declared. "I'm going to magick it away."

She refrained from asking whether this made it sexual. It honestly didn't matter, as that desire which flowed so freely before was still absent.

Her toga disappeared, leaving her naked against the cool fabric of the bed. She glanced back, but she could feel Leksander still had his clothes, as the rough fabric of his jeans brushed against her skin.

But this time, when he leaned forward, and his hands met her back, the sensation was entirely different. Skin-to-skin, their magic—dragon and angel—always sparked in a tense interplay. A small skirmish of magic where they touched, electrifying her skin… and warming other parts as well. This time, when his fingers moved rhythmically, coaxing the muscles of her back to give and move, her body responded.

She could hear Leksander's breath—sharp intakes and long outtakes—but her eyes had fallen shut with the pleasure. And it *was* pleasure. Along her shoulders, down her back, then up the sides again. But it was a different sort than she'd experienced before with him. It was not unlike being strung up with black satin ribbon. Leksander was completely in control. He pushed and moved; her body followed and responded. His touch was strong, and his fingers worked deep. She could feel that relaxation he wished for steal over her body, releasing cares and worries from every inch, not just the ones he touched. It was as if he possessed a strange magic that pulled concerns out from every part of her via the probing, stroking, pressure points on her back.

A small moan escaped her.

Leksander's hands became more fervent in their quest.

Her body felt as though it were melting into the bed. She'd never felt such complete and utter loss of tension except... except after Leksander had brought her to a wing-shaking climax that left her limp afterward. *Sated.* But this was different. She was almost immobilized from the relaxation, yet the sensation of letting go was perversely making her sensitive, sexual parts—between her legs, her breasts mashed into the bed—come alive.

Leksander rumbled a small groan as he moved his attention to her bottom, massaging deep into the rounded flesh. She had no verbal response—she was so captured by the puddle of relaxation she had become—but her body squirmed of its own volition. The ache between her legs was growing, and the wish to have him touch her *there* was driving her mad.

Leksander sucked in a breath, and it came out as a shudder. She felt it vibrate through his arms and into his hands on her bottom. Then he lifted one hand free. She was about to complain that he shouldn't stop, when the feeling of rough fabric against her skin disappeared, replaced by the cool press of bare flesh. He leaned forward, covering her body with his.

Leksander was a hard man all over—well-muscled and strong—but there was no mistaking the stiff rod of his cock now pressing into her back.

He brushed her hair away from her face, where it had

fallen. "I was wrong," he whispered hoarsely in her ear. "This is entirely sexual." He caressed her bottom, no longer kneading it with his massaging touch but enlivening it with his fingertips. "Tell me to stop." He gripped her bottom, hard.

She could hardly speak, rendered senseless by the relaxation and speechless by the surge in desire flooding every part of her body. She licked her lips, eyes still closed, and managed, "Don't stop."

Leksander growled and released his hold on her bottom then slipped his hand between her legs.

She gasped. *Sweet angels of light.* The mere brush of his fingertips on the wet heat there made her body jolt.

"Oh, fuck, yes." Leksander's voice had dropped into a growl that excited her even more. But then he withdrew his hand and slid his body lower on hers. Just as she was trying to form words—any words—to get him to return to the delicate torment between her legs, he reached around instead, slipping his hand between her body and the bed, lifting her slightly. He found her most sensitive spot with expert precision, and his fingers danced across her aching flesh.

She gasped. Then his cock slid deliciously between her legs, somehow finding her entrance and filling her with one long stroke. *"Gah,"* she cried out as he buried himself inside her.

He held still, a muffled cry of his own. She was so relaxed and so completely filled, this felt like the perfect state. One she could stay in forever and be utterly satisfied. But then Leksander flicked his fingers on her sensitive spot again, and suddenly she was squirming underneath him, bucking up and craving him to move.

"Hold still," Leksander commanded, then he pressed his hand to the flat of her back, pushing her deeper into the bed. Once he had her fixed there, he drew back and thrust in deep.

So deep. She cried out again on the second thrust. The third and fourth had her whimpering. Leksander's grunts and groans and the wild way he pounded just spiked the pleasure running rampant like an electric storm throughout her body. His name escaped her lips, again and again, and he took her, full and deep and powerful. Every stroke had her crying out now, but then he just picked up the pace, possessing her with more fury. A deep and guttural scream finally ripped out of her, turning to angel-song as her body clenched and convulsed and bucked up into him.

He cried out too, then slammed deep and stayed there. She felt his hot seed spilling, the twitching of his cock inside her, and the ripple throughout his whole body, now heavy on top of hers.

"Holy fuck. Holy, holy fuck." His words were whispers, and he seemed to try to move away from her body but failed. Then he just pushed back the hair that had fallen on her face and kissed her there—cheeks, ear, hair, and down her neck to her shoulder. "Just when I think," he breathed between kisses, "that sex with you can't get any hotter, you blow my mind, angel girl."

She struggled to make her mouth functional again, not just hang open, panting. "Just wait until it's your turn, dragon prince."

"Oh, God, yes," he prayed, his forehead pressed into her back as he seemed to still work on recovering his breath. Then he pulled back, finally leaving her body, and fell breathless on the bed next to her. His hand lingered on her back, just keeping a connection between them, but his eyes were closed, and his breath was ragged.

She recovered faster, perhaps because his lovemaking

had truly brought back her joy. This man—this good and righteous man—was the father of the child inside her. She was imperfect, but she carried perfection—her angel nature—as her birthright. Between them, they couldn't have formed anything less than the spotless soul she felt pulsing inside her womb. So come what may in the dark future ahead, Leksander was right—if she could survive this, if she was strong enough to give this baby life, then she would have done something *good.*

She wouldn't doubt it again.

Erelah edged up on her side and curled up next to Leksander's splayed body. His eyes were still closed, and her light touch on his chest—just fingertips resting there— seemed to jolt him awake.

"Have I exhausted you, dragon prince?" She grinned. In truth, he did all the work. But she could fix that next time.

A slow smile spread across his face, then he opened his eyes and slid a sideways glance to her. "Is that an invitation?"

"I think you are too sluggish with pleasure." She sat upright on the bed.

He scowled at her. *"Sluggish?"*

"The bed has made you soft," she teased, edging up onto her knees. "And slow." She twisted fast and scrambled off the bed. His hands closed on her bottom to yank her back, but she slipped from his grasp. She heard his growl but didn't look back as she dashed to the furthest corner from the bed, up against the conjured rock wall that blocked the mouth of the cave.

He was right behind her, and when she turned, he grabbed her wrists and pinned them above her head to the wall. *"Slow?"* he growled, a wicked smile on his face. "I'll show you slow."

That promise of sweet torment was almost too good to pass up. Still, she was tempted to pulse a little angel power and blast him across the room, just to make him work for it.

But then the wall shook behind her. At the same time, something *boomed.*

Blank surprise took over her face.

Leksander stepped back, eyes wide. "What was that?"

She shook her head, rapidly, and fear seized her.

Leksander waved a hand at the rocky wall, wiping it from existence. The white curtain lay in shreds, charred on the floor.

And beyond the mouth of the cave lay a horrible destruction.

Chapter Four

HOLY SHIT. FOR A MOMENT, LEKSANDER WAS FROZEN IN place.

Then he rushed forward to the mouth of the cave, remembering at the last moment to stop before getting burned by its magical electric energy.

Outside, chaos filled the skies. Swarms of shadow angelings, their dark wings glistening in the sun, dipped and wove in the air above the canyon. The rocky walls on either side were likewise coated with black-winged creatures clinging to the rock, awaiting their turn to take flight. The dragons of the House of Smoke... *his brothers...* they were nowhere to be seen.

Then Leksander spied a black dragon, broken and bloodied, being carried by two shadow angelings just before they flipped in the air and disappeared—carrying that dragon off to some horrible fate in the shadow realm.

"Nooo!" Leksander shouted his frustration, but that only caught the attention of one of the shadow angelings. He paused mid-air, baring his teeth, which were filed to sharp points. He had an unearthly beauty, like all the angelings—shadow or light—but the snarl and the teeth and the twisted, black tattoos across his chest turned him into a terror. Then he rushed at the cave—

Leksander stumbled back, catching Erelah behind him and pulling her close.

The shadow angel bashed into the wards at full speed —and bounced. He shrieked, and a trail of sparks and smoke tumbled with him to the bottom of the canyon.

"Leksander." Erelah's voice trembled. She was clutching her stomach.

"What's wrong?" The terror that gripped him now had nothing to do with the shadow angelings outside and everything to do with the angeling he loved.

"The baby." Her deep scowl reached inside him and carved its mark. "It is…" She searched for the word. *"Angry."*

What? Leksander gripped her shoulders and tugged her back from the cave mouth. They were both still naked, so he quickly conjured clothes. "What do you mean?"

Erelah was rubbing her belly. Her eyes had fallen shut. "It's all right," she murmured. "They cannot harm you." She was speaking to their baby, reassuring him.

"They can't penetrate the wards," he assured her… and the baby. Somehow, the tiny thing had been upset by what was happening outside. Or maybe the baby sensed that Erelah was upset. Either way, Leksander was freaking out enough for the both of them… and he needed to keep his head about this.

Then another *boom* rocked the cave, vibrating the floor and stirring the dust.

Erelah's eyes popped open and scanned the chaos outside.

Then Leksander saw what the swarms of angelings were trying to accomplish. They were picking up rocks—

boulders really—and carrying them to the top of the canyon, above the cave… and then dropping them.

"Holy shit," he whispered, his brain stunned once again.

Both his brothers, *gone.* A dozen of the House of Smoke's best warriors, *gone.* Who the hell knew what happened to Tajael. And now these shadow angelings were trying to *bomb* their way into his cave.

"How close are we to the top?" Erelah asked quickly.

"Too close." He scoured his memories. "Maybe twenty feet of rock? Maybe less." *Shit!* Why hadn't he found some-place more secure?

"We have to leave." But her eyes were as wide as his.

"We *can't* leave!" Leksander scrubbed his face. *Think.* What could they do?

"You drop the wards, and I open a door—"

"It's too risky."

Another boom rocked the cave. *"This* is too risky!"

Oh, fuck. She was probably right, but *holy, magic,* this had gone bad fast.

Even though they were further back in the cave, they had caught the attention of two more angelings. One flew at them, headlong, like the first had, only to be knocked senseless by the wards. The second hovered in front of the cave opening, studying it… and them. Then he spread his wings and lifted out of sight.

"That's not good." Leksander bit his lip then turned to Erelah. "You don't even have a blade, my love."

"It matters not," she replied quickly. "If I have to fight with a blade, we are lost. The numbers are too great." She grimaced. "And I recognize this Regiment."

Leksander nodded. "The tattoos are the same. These are Elyon's angelings." Elyon was the sworn enemy of Razael, Erelah's angel father, who turned shadow at her conception. Elyon already had a special interest in Erelah and had tried to kill her once. At least once.

"If his angelings are here, he cannot be far behind," Erelah said.

Another swarm of angelings caught their attention. The black-winged creatures were working together, carrying what looked like a tree between them, barreling down the canyon.

"What the fuck are they doing?" Leksander asked, mouth gaping.

"They are…" Erelah gasped. "They are coming *here.*"

The cohort of angelings was picking up speed, and it was clear they intended to ram the invisible wards with this massive uprooted tree they had scavenged from somewhere in the forest. But the wards were only meant to keep out immortal beings and magic. Not flying missile trees. "Look out!" he shouted, but Erelah had already unfurled her wings and leaped to the top of the cave, jumping free of the path of the tree. At the last instant, Leksander scrambled to conjure a rock wall to block it. The trunk of the tree sailed into the cave, roots first—the wall formed a fraction of a second too late, slicing the tree in half. The massive root ball crashed in Leksander, carrying him to smash into the back wall. The force was a fraction of what it would have been with the full tree, but it was still so hard that he nearly blacked out. Both he and the mass of roots slumped to the floor.

He was dazed at first but managed to shove it off then scramble on hands and knees through the mess. "Erelah!" He climbed over the root tangle, searching for her. *"Erelah!"* There was no answer, but the damn wall was in the way. He waved it away, revealing a tree explosion in the front half of the cave. Erelah was standing at the front in a corner made by the wards and the massive tree trunk, which was sticking right through them. She was apparently unharmed—*thank God*—but she was talking to someone just outside.

A shadow angeling.

What the fuck? "Don't listen to him!" Leksander yelled out as he climbed over roots and shattered tree pieces, bracing himself against the trunk that crowded the cave. He struggled to keep his footing as he made his way to the front.

The shadow angeling flicked a look to him, dropped something at the edge of the cave, and then lifted off. For a moment, Leksander could see dark markings in long stripes across his back. Not the normal tattoos, these looked like healed-over wounds, ropy and jagged. The angeling soared up out of view.

"Are you okay?" Leksander asked Erelah when he reached her, his hands automatically gripping her shoulders, his gaze scanning her body. But she didn't have a scratch.

"I'm fine," she said tersely. "But we must leave, Leksander."

"Who the hell was that?" he asked, jerking his thumb toward the shadow angeling who just left.

"He is Elyon's son." When his eyes bugged out, she added, "His name is Micah. He helped free me from his father before."

Leksander scowled. "I thought Tajael rescued you."

"Him as well." She peered down at the lip of the cave, just outside the wards. "But we can trust Micah. He paid a price for his help, one he knew was coming. He has a pure heart, even in shadow. And besides… he has brought me a blade."

Leksander followed her gaze. Sure enough, there was a

black-as-midnight angel blade on the narrow ledge. "Why would he do that?"

She frowned. "I don't really understand it. But he does not wish to follow Elyon's ways."

Leksander shook his head. *Whatever.* The masses of shadow angelings were still churning the sky. "Even with a blade, I don't know about this, my love." He knew what she wanted—to lower the wards and run. "Even if we reach the keep and no one follows..." He turned to face her. *"Which they will.* It takes time to lower the wards at the keep and then raise them again. Not a lot of time, but precious seconds we may not have if we have angelings on our heels."

She scowled, looked to the knife, then back out at the forces gathered. "Or angels."

He blinked. "What?" Then he looked. At the far side of the canyon, another black-winged form had appeared, but this one was larger than the others. Leksander could hear his rolling, dark laugh across the canyon. His hair was white and long and floated out like an unholy halo from his head. "Elyon," he whispered.

"We must leave *now,"* Erelah rushed out. "Drop the wards. I shall grab the blade. Should any reach us before I can travel—with you by my side—then I can fight them. Or if they follow us to the keep."

Leksander nodded, his chest tight. He'd gone after Erelah when Elyon captured her the first time. Leksander had been the bait that lured a legion of dark angelings away from her. A distraction. But a True Angel was more powerful than a legion of angelings put together—and while it seemed like his wards should hold against any immortal, he'd only ever seen it tested with ordinary immortals like angelings and dragons. Even the fae were nothing to the full power of a True Angel.

If Elyon wanted to batter down the wards... it was possible he could.

"All right," Leksander said, quickly. "Are you ready?"

She edged closer to where the blade lay just outside the wards. Then she bent down, ready to grab it. She took his hand and peered up at him. "Ready, my love."

His heart clenched. A full scrum of dark angelings and a Dark Angel himself were outside those wards... and he was about to bring them down. Exposing his mate and the child who was the urgent target of everyone. Leksander swallowed and raised his hand—

"What is that?" he asked, freezing his hand mid-air. Another black-winged angel had appeared above Elyon... along with easily a hundred angelings at his back.

Erelah popped back up, scowling. Then her eyes went wide. "It's my father!"

Leksander grimaced. Razael was far better than Elyon, but he was still an angel in shadow... and he probably had his own ideas about this baby his daughter was carrying.

"We should still go," Leksander said, squeezing her hand.

"No, wait." Her attention was captured by the fight unfolding. It was like a giant vacuum had sucked every angeling out of the air near the cave entrance and pulled them toward the mid-air standoff at the opposite side of the canyon.

"*Now*, while they're distracted," Leksander insisted.

Erelah bit her lip, but she didn't respond. They both watched as the sky blackened with dark wings. This battle would be epic, and bloody, and a hell of a distraction for them to escape under. Maybe it would be better to wait until they went at it.

And then in a blink... Elyon was gone. Along with his angeling hordes.

Vanished without a sound or spilling a single drop of angeling blood.

"Okay, what just happened?" Leksander felt like all of this—the entirety of his time in this cave with Erelah—was one insanity after the next.

"I don't know." The blank surprise on her face mirrored his.

"I *still* think we should go," he said.

She turned to him, placing a hand on his chest. "My father is an angel Fallen because he created *me.*" She blinked a little too much then shook her head. "It matters less that he is *my* father. The fact that he was trying to create an angeling without Falling... don't you see? He *must* know more about this. He must have had a plan for how to bring me into the world—just like our child—without bringing the End of Times."

"The End of—*Erelah!*" He gave her an exasperated look. "That's not your responsibility. You need only worry about *our* baby. Our family."

"You are wrong, dragon prince."

But before he could argue any further, Razael appeared next to them in a flash of angel light. Leksander stumbled back, dragging Erelah with him. She was nowhere near as concerned about this as he was.

"Erelah." The angel's voice boomed. He was ungodly beautiful—long dark hair, bright blue eyes—demon-like but less than Elyon and his minions. "Is it true? Are you carrying this dragon's child?"

Erelah stood straighter. "Yes."

"And your wings?" As he floated there, grilling Erelah with questions, his hundred angelings had followed him across the canyon and formed a cloud of black feathers in the air around him.

"Why do you care?" Leksander asked. He didn't like the direction this was going.

But Erelah had already unfurled them, and their snowy white beauty was cramped by the tree trunk bisecting the cave.

Razael sighed and briefly closed his eyes. A murmur of awe or appreciation or something went through the assembled angelings. And a few icy looks as well—those made the hairs on the back of Leksander's neck rise. He stepped in front of Erelah, a reflexive protection, even though it was no doubt useless.

"You are truly earning your name, Aurora," her father said.

Leksander threw a pinched look at Erelah.

"The name he had chosen for me before I was born," she explained. To her father, she said, "How have you banished Elyon? We need to make transit to Leksander's keep to ensure the baby will be safe until it's ready to be born. Then… then we can talk, my father. There is much I have need of learning from you."

Even Leksander could see that soften the angel's heart. Leksander still didn't trust him, but if Razael could safeguard them on their way to the keep…

"This dragon's wards will not be sufficient to hold Elyon off, my child." He frowned. "Not if he knows you have returned to the light. Above all, he wishes to see that destroyed. To see you in shadow. Then you will be nothing but another disgraced angeling who tried to mate and stay pure of heart. You are no threat then—indeed, you are an asset to the shadow realm. On pain of battle with me—a battle that would have incurred massive losses on his side and mine, for he knows how I feel for you—he agreed to let me be the one to turn you. But turn you, I must. Or he will come for you."

"You're not turning anyone," Leksander said, stepping even further back from the wards and grasping hold of Erelah's hand. He would love her in light or in shadow—that didn't matter—but he'd be damned if he'd let some fallen angel decide that for her.

"It's all right," Erelah said.

He turned to her. "No. It's not." He dropped his voice even though surely the angel could hear. "You don't know his intention, Erelah."

She put a hand to his cheek. "But I *do* know. He tried to stay in the light when he created me, Leksander. He attempted to do what we are doing now. I'm carrying the child he thought I could be. He knows how this could possibly work. Please. Trust me on this."

There was no part of him that liked this. "It's not that I don't trust *you*—"

"He doesn't trust *me*, Erelah," her father said from behind him. "And with good reason."

Leksander turned to scowl at him.

Razael offered up his hands. "I told Elyon I would turn her to shadow. But I have no intention of doing so, dragon prince. If Erelah can remain in the light, then that must be allowed to happen. That's why you must come to my Regiment for the duration of the pregnancy. She will be well hidden there." He gestured around to the angelings floating beside him. "We can offer protection you can get nowhere else."

"He is right," Erelah said quickly. "We should go. Before Elyon suspects that my father has failed."

What the fuck… this was the most insane idea he'd heard in a day of insanity.

But he also couldn't see a way around it.

"We'll have more time to talk once we're safely away," Razael added. He floated back from the wards, waiting.

Erelah looked to Leksander, expectant.

"Fine." He prayed he wasn't making a horrible mistake.

Then he raised his hand and wiped away the wards.

Razael held out his hand, beckoning them. His angelings didn't rush in. Razael didn't charge them. They simply waited for Leksander and Erelah to make the next move.

Erelah swept forward, retrieved her obsidian blade from the edge of the cave, then stepped back to grasp hold of Leksander's hand.

Then she twisted, and the familiar squeeze of inter-dimensional travel clamped down on Leksander's body.

They were going to the shadow realm.

Chapter Five

Erelah landed on her father's balcony, Leksander in tow.

The black crystal beneath her bare feet was cool on her heated skin, and the vast cavern of her father's Regiment in the shadow realm was empty—but only for a moment. The air popped and light flashed, announcing the arrival of Razael's entire contingent. Over a hundred angelings, their dark wings setting an immediate whisper throughout the tall, slender space. Her father's oversized shadow angel form alit on the balcony next to her and Leksander.

Erelah wasted no time, simply dragged Leksander by the hand indoors. She'd stowed away her snowy white wings, but with all this dark energy around her, the angeling child in her womb was pulsing its tiny energy. Anger. Distress. Alarm. Erelah wasn't sure what the tremors in energy meant, but they'd zoomed up when Leksander had dropped the wards, and the full shadow energy of her father's Regiment washed over her.

"It's all right, little one," she whispered. She had no

idea if her words carried any weight. The child trembled on.

Leksander was giving her quizzical looks, but he held fast by her side, slipping an arm around her waist once she stopped at the back of the receiving room. She hesitated to descend further into her father's labyrinthine crystal palace, waiting instead for her father to follow her from the balcony. He hoarsely called out instructions to his Regiment then tucked his vast wings to enter the room.

She held her dark blade—the one she had fashioned, Razael had blessed, and Micah had returned to her—at her side. Not that she would have need of it here.

"Erelah." Her father said her name like it was made of relief. "I'm so glad you chose this for your Sanctuary."

"How safe is she here, truly?" Leksander's hand gently squeezed her waist. "Elyon came here before for her."

"And he will again." Razael tipped his head. "If he suspects she remains in the light."

Erelah frowned—part of this didn't make sense. "Elyon is truly in shadow. He craves the chaos and violence and bloodshed of his breed. If my baby—born of angeling, made of light—will bring about the Great Fall, the End of Times... why would he not welcome that?"

Razael lifted his eyebrows and nodded. "So you've thought it through."

"What is this End of Times you keep talking about?" Leksander demanded. "All I know is our child will renew the treaty. He will keep humanity safe from the fae for another five hundred years. That's a *good* thing, Erelah." He was speaking directly to her now.

"It's by no means certain that the Fall will come," Razael agreed.

"See?" Leksander said, but that was nowhere near enough explanation for her.

"You must not have thought so," Erelah said to her father, carefully, "if you were determined to be the first in creating me and staying in the light." Her father was a True Angel—in theory, he should have wisdom and knowledge that surpass anything an angeling can hope to obtain. And yet… he fell in love with her mother. He contrived to get her with child. Was he overcome by his Sin of Lust… rendered senseless with True Love… or did he truly understand what he was attempting?

Razael stepped closer. His oversized body loomed above her, and his flexed dark wings stretched the width of the receiving room. Her child pulsed magic, and it wasn't a joyful kind. More a reflex—his angeling-of-light magic clashing against her father's shadow darkness. Razael frowned and dropped his gaze to her belly.

"This angeling has your strength and your spirit, Erelah." Angels were cool and aloof—angels of light, at least—but pure human-like emotion warred across her father's face. "You were the same, from the first moment you were created. You rebelled against me when I Fell. I could feel your turmoil, the ancient reflex of light battling dark, even in your mother's womb. It was part of why I left."

Erelah scowled. "I thought you left because you couldn't control your shadow urges."

Leksander dashed a look at her, but she was focused on her father's troubled face. If she was in danger here—if her father posed a threat to her child—she would leave in an instant. And bring Leksander with her. Razael knew that.

Her father nodded. "That was a concern as well. Once unleashed, my Lust was near unquenchable with your mother around."

Erelah arched an eyebrow and glanced at Leksander.

She remembered that uncontrolled feeling—that Lust spinning urgently out of control, both for her as angeling and for him as wyvern. For him, it was simply a matter of reining in the beast. For her, the True Love she had for Leksander tamed it. Lust and Love merged and became something holy—in the light. She was already ahead of what her father had managed. That thought sparked a dangerous surge of Pride. She tamped that down and focused on the problem at hand.

Surviving. Bringing her child into the world. Not causing the destruction of all humanity.

Razael lifted his hands to encompass her and Leksander. "I will provide a room for you during your internment. One with privacy for all the sexual activity you might require."

"Internment?" Leksander asked with suspicion.

Erelah scowled but not at Leksander's worry. They were not *trapped* here. But the idea of an entire pregnancy spent in passion with Leksander locked away in a room deep in the shadow realm... would her Lust drive her to shadow, given time? What would happen to her baby then? Perhaps being in shadow—failing to stay in the light—would avoid the temptation she would present to all angels of light. But would her child survive it? He was already fighting the nearness of the shadow forces all around her. Would he fight against his own mother?

She stepped back from her father.

Leksander moved between them as if he could protect her with his body. She was certain it was a purely reflexive move. His great and good soul was at heart Protector Class, just like her.

"First," Erelah said to her father, "I need to know more about all of this. How angelings in shadow are born. What you thought my birth would bring. How likely it is that angels will attempt this, should I succeed. And will it bring the End?"

Her father tipped his head to her. "All crucial questions. Are you sure you wouldn't rather retire and rest and perhaps have sex?"

Erelah scowled. This obsession he had with her and Leksander's lovemaking was unseemly. And suspicious. Did he think this would turn her to shadow? Was that his true aim here, not just a false promise to Elyon? That she would turn and then remain in the shadow realm? It wasn't as if her father loved the light. Not anymore. She and Leksander exchanged a look, and indeed, she wished she were alone with him to talk freely. But she could tell his concerns were hers.

"No, I wish to discuss this *now.*" Erelah left no room for negotiation in her voice.

"Very well." Razael sighed. "There is deep chaos at work in all the realms, Erelah."

She narrowed her eyes. "There's a demon uprising in Seattle."

"Is there?" Razael seemed surprised, but his expression quickly settled into a scowl. "Then there is even more afoot than I knew."

"The demons are the work of a fae from the Winter Court," Leksander explained to her father. "Zephan is using vampires to get around the treaty and infect humans with demon essence." Then he frowned at Erelah. "Once the treaty renews, the House of Smoke and angels of light can give that their full focus, right? I mean, it's tangentially related to all this… but not really."

"The two cannot be as separate as you think," Razael said.

Leksander seemed confused.

But Erelah nodded. "When I was captured by Elyon, he mentioned the fae. Said that they wanted to kill me as if he were tasked with delivering me unto them. I thought he meant the summer queen, and I hoped he would." Leksander seemed startled, so she explained, "Her cage would have been preferable to the torment Elyon had in mind for me."

Leksander's expression shifted to one ready to tear the wings off an angel, never mind the impossibility of that.

"It is imperative that I not be captured by Elyon again," Erelah added. "He would destroy the child and me. If we must stay here to avoid that, then that is what we'll have to do."

Leksander's jaw worked like he was holding back words. Finally, he said, "Agreed."

"Elyon might do even worse than destroy you, Erelah," her father said.

"I'm certain he would defile me as well," Erelah said stiffly. "But it would be death in the end."

Her father's face wrestled with emotion again. "There are several possible unhappy outcomes when it comes to Elyon. If he's truly working with the fae—and that sounds very like him, allying with the most hated enemy of the light—it would be with the Winter Court. They would likely just kill you and the baby without making a spectacle of it."

"Zephan's already tried to destroy my brother's mates," Leksander growled.

"But if Elyon had you," Razael continued, "he might not give you up so easily. He might simply steal the baby, even before it is born."

"*What?*" Erelah's heart seized. "He would take it..."

Her words stalled out, her mind refusing to envision that horror.

"Why would he do such a thing?" Leksander looked equally horrified.

"Why do the shadow steal from the light?" Razael spit out. "Because they can. Because it brings them pleasure. And being angel, Elyon has powers over life that exceed anything you're prepared to face, dragon. He would take this child and claim it for his own, implanting it in one of his dark angelings for host and raising it in shadow." He turned to Erelah. "And he knows what you mean to me, Aurora. He would do it just to break what's left of a tired angel's heart."

"Clearly, this must not happen." Erelah was trying to keep calm, but the baby was pulsing his magic again, and even she could hear the tremble in her voice.

Leksander's arm slid around her shoulders, and he held her close.

"And it won't under my protection," her father vowed.

Once again, her father seemed a little too strident. Perhaps he was right. But it was also possible he wished to keep her in his Regiment, hoping she would turn. "What if I became shadow? What would happen to the baby?"

Razael seemed startled by this. "Well, we would make a home for you both…"

"So the baby would be born in shadow." Could she do that to her own child? The idea made chills race down her back.

Razael frowned. "All angelings are born in light. Which is why the mothers are so often kidnapped, stolen away and hidden until they give birth. Just as Markos stole your mother away, once you were conceived, and I had gone shadow. I returned for you and your mother, hoping I could bring you with me, but you were gone. Whoever claims the child, controls its fate. Markos claimed you. Thus you remained in the light of your birth."

Erelah couldn't tell if he counted this as a positive outcome or not.

"And if my child is born of light and I remain in light?" she asked.

"Then you will usher in a new age for angelkind." He scowled. "One that may see a resurgence of the light over shadow as angels of light build up their armies and squash shadow once and for all… or one that may see the angels of light Fall in unprecedented numbers, tipping the balance forever into dark."

Erelah swallowed. "There is no way to know?"

"I thought it certain that you couldn't return to the light, my daughter," he said softly. "You seem determined to break all the rules."

That, finally, gave her some measure of hope. Because he was right—she had done something no one else had. Except for Tajael, but when he went shadow, he had not yet made his vows. She had not only made them, she'd broken them. Thoroughly. Only through the grace of Leksander's True Love had she came back to the light.

Her hand sought his, and she smiled. "It's going to be all right."

His shoulders seemed to relax, finally. "We're going to *make* it be all right." Then he kissed her, just softly on the cheek, but it felt like a direct injection of his love. And suddenly, she couldn't wait to find a room in the warrens of her father's palace, a place where she could be alone with her love and show him all the ways she loved him. Sequestered so, she could easily spend the weeks that must ensue to grow this child.

She turned back to Razael. "If it pleases you, father, we would—"

A warrior's cry sounded outside, cutting her off and jolting alarm through her body. *That was no warrior of shadow…* Her father turned, his wings nearly swiping them from their feet in his haste to return to the balcony. Erelah surged forward to go after him, but Leksander held her back.

"Whatever this is, we need to *hide,* not run to our deaths," he said.

"But that's not…" She trailed off as it became clear through the open door exactly who had arrived in her father's Regiment—*Markos and Tajael.* They stood on the balcony below a swirling vortex of shadow angelings, facing her shadow angel father.

"Oh, fuck," Leksander spat.

But this might not be the terrible thing he assumed. "Come," she beckoned him toward the door. "Let us make peace before there is bloodshed."

"What are they *doing* here?" he asked.

She gave him a scowl. *Of course,* they were here for her. Then she strode out onto the balcony. Markos may be an angel, and thus able to control every aspect of his appearance, but Tajael was just an angeling—one who appeared to have been beaten near to death. Or perhaps stabbed. He had shadow wounds on every limb, and a dark, ragged gash across his chest.

But when he saw her, his face lit up. "Thank the heavens, you're alive!" Such was his joy that Erelah couldn't help but return his fervent smile.

"She belongs in my Dominion," Markos was saying to Razael.

Her father's face was alive with fury. "She is safer here."

"Hardly." Markos had barely spared a flick of a look in her direction, but she understood why—his entire attention was devoted to the dark angel in front of him. He was prepared to go to war over her. A surge of Pride once again gushed through her. It felt as if it were lifting her feet from the balcony. Taming it this time was almost impossible, especially with Tajael shoving his way past the angel staring contest to rush to her side.

"Are you well? Is the baby unharmed?" he rushed out.

For some reason, her Pride was choking her. True, she had spent decades hoping to shine bright enough with Virtue to earn Markos's approval. And also true that she thought all of that lost when she had gone shadow. And further true that the faction leader's approval was a pale reflection of the righteousness of being a True Angel, but it was the most angelings could hope for.

Yet it was still surprising, the surge of emotion—*Markos came for her. Personally.*

"She was *fine*, Tajael," Leksander said. "Until you showed up."

Tajael gave him an almost comical look. "But we're here to bring her to Sanctuary."

Leksander dropped his voice. "Yeah, well, you're about to start a war."

And it was true—Markos had spread his wings, and Razael seemed ready to take the fight into the air as well.

Erelah finally found her voice. "Wait!" She strode forward, ignoring Leksander and Tajael's attempts to hold her back. "Do not fight over me!" Those words surged more Pride, but then something unexpected happened. When she had crossed only half the balcony, still a dozen feet from the angels of light and dark, the child inside her pulsed a fury of angel power. She stumbled, gripping her stomach. It didn't *hurt* so much—more like her midsection was *vibrating* with the power. Churning and nauseous and stopping her cold in her tracks.

"What's wrong?" Razael said, lurching closer.

Markos likewise stepped toward her. "This place is foul for the child."

"What?" Razael said. "Fuck off, Markos."

The baby's power surged again. This time Erelah cried out and nearly doubled over.

"What is happening?" That was Leksander at her back, holding her and bending with her.

"The baby," she gasped. She looked up at the fury on both her father's faces—the one who gave her life and the one who brought her to the light.

"Move back!" Tajael ordered, but he wasn't speaking to her—his command was for Markos and Razael. Even in Tajael's bruised and battered state, her valiant friend, the avowed protector of her child, was putting himself between Erelah and the light and dark angels before her. "Your war is a torment for the child. Can't you see that?" And surely they could, as angels are better at perceiving things of the soul than even angelings.

Leksander was dragging her backward, toward the receiving room. But she couldn't allow them to fight over her. "Wait!" she whispered hoarsely to him. They had gained enough distance from Markos and Razael that the baby had quieted. She straightened up from her hunched position, now that the nausea had abated somewhat.

"I will bring a hundred angelings of light to your rescue, Erelah," Markos declared, both to her and to Razael. "A thousand. I will make allegiance with every angel of light in God's kingdom rather than leave you in shadow."

Oh, the Pride! It surged even stronger than her baby's angel power.

Her father wore his distress like fury. "You'll lose a thousand and more!"

"No!" Erelah's voice rang out. She raised her hands as if in benediction over them, to keep them at peace. "You will not make war over me. Or my child." To her father, she said, "That would only plunge us both into shadow, father. And I want to give my baby a chance—a chance at the light."

She could see the heartbreak on his face, but it was Truth, and she was vowed to Truth in all things now. It was part of what kept her out of the darkness. To Markos, she said, "Do not call your warriors. I will go with you and Tajael."

She looked to Leksander—she had made this decision without him, but he was nodding his approval. He had one hand on the small of her back and the other on her elbow, steadying her. She still had her shadow angel blade in her hand, and that wouldn't be welcome in Markos's Dominion.

She handed it over to Tajael. "Give this to my father." As he did so, she said to him, "Someday, my father, I hope to see you return to the light. Until this baby comes, however things turn out, the light is where I need to be."

Razael accepted the blade. Gripping it, he gave her a long, wordless look. She didn't quite understand the emotions she saw splaying across his face, but before she could say any more, he lifted from the balcony, summoning his Regiment of dark angelings to fly to the top of his cavern, leaving only angels and angelings of light and a single dragon on the balcony.

"That was a wise choice, Erelah." Somehow Markos's approval felt tarnished by the lingering sadness her father left behind.

"It is for the best," Tajael added. He was back by her side. "Do you need assistance?" he asked as if she were crippled by carrying this tiny spark of a child, barely a day old. But now that her father had departed, and the tension had eased, the baby was quiet again.

"I remember the way home," Erelah said with a small smile.

She gripped Leksander's hand in hers and twisted time and space to take her there.

Chapter Six

LEKSANDER STUMBLED AS THEY LANDED IN THE TRAINING chamber of Markos's Dominion.

He had hoped Erelah would take them straight to her cell—he was desperate for time alone with her. But he could see the logic. This was neutral territory, of sorts. Markos's throne room would show she was fully back in the fold. Her cell would be uncomfortably tight with all four of them… plus Leksander didn't want either Markos or Tajael in what was essentially Erelah's bedchamber. Not that he was jealous of them, but she *was* his mate. This was *their* child. For all the fighting going on to "claim" Erelah as a member of the light or dark, it was *his* mark she carried on her back.

Which made it painful when she kissed Tajael.

Leksander knew it was a life kiss, and any fool could see the angeling needed it—he had dark, inky wounds all over his body—but dammit, he didn't like *watching* it. Markos looked on with cool approval, inscrutable the way True Angels usually were. But he seemed pleased to be back in his domain with his prize. It *might* be safer here—fuck if

Leksander really knew anything at this point—but it still ground his gears to see that smug expression on Markos's face.

Holy fuck, that life kiss was going on forever.

He was about to break it up when Erelah released the angeling, and Tajael stumbled free.

"That was unnecessary," Tajael breathed, but Leksander knew exactly how he felt. Elated. Riding a high like no other. *Alive* in a way no one normally experienced. At least, that's how it felt when Erelah had given *him* a life kiss and brought him back from the wounds inflicted by Elyon's dark angelings.

And now he *was* fucking jealous. And not of the high.

"Of course it was." Erelah was shaking her head at Tajael. "You're lucky to have escaped with your life."

Leksander strode over to slide his arm around Erelah's shoulder. It was a possessive move, but the way she melted into him, arm around his back, hand on his chest... it was like she was feeling the same thing. The need to touch—to *connect*—again.

He nuzzled into her hair. "How far is it to your cell?" he asked, voice already husky. He'd only been to Markos's Dominion a few times and didn't have the layout memorized.

She peered at him, confusion writ on her face.

Okay, maybe they weren't thinking *exactly* the same thing...

"I have something for you, Erelah." Markos produced an angel blade from somewhere in his spare angel toga.

To Leksander's chagrin, she escaped from his touch to go retrieve it.

The blade seemed to hum, and she smiled. "You've blessed it," she gushed. *The look on her face...* Leksander had seen it time and again, and it always spurred a jealous knot in his stomach. *She adored Markos.* It was clear to anyone with eyes. Leksander used to think it was sexual, despite what he'd heard about angels and angelings not fucking each other. But not that long ago he'd witnessed a kiss between her and Tajael he took for something *very* sexual. He'd been mistaken about that, and he wasn't sure why now, of all times, his jealousy was spiking, and he was questioning Markos's intentions regarding Erelah again.

Maybe because, this time, she was Leksander's *mate.*

Maybe because, this time, he knew Markos *wanted* something from her. Badly.

Maybe because angelings having sex and staying in the light had never been a real possibility before, but here Erelah stood, gorgeous and womanly and pregnant with a world-changing baby… and Markos was feasting on her with his eyes.

Fucking angels. "Okay, thanks for the blade," Leksander said, bringing Erelah back under his arm again. "We shouldn't need it here, right? You're supposed to protect us." He definitely put the *us* in there on purpose. In case Markos got any ideas about Leksander now being an expendable piece of this equation.

"The danger is still considerable," Tajael said. His face was glowing from the life kiss, and the inky shadow markings had vanished. "But we'll be more prepared now than at the cave." He glanced Markos and seemed hesitant to elaborate.

But that was *Leksander's* House that took a beating. "What *did* happen there? Erelah and I were a little busy, just the two of us." He threw a pointed look at Markos so he would be clear on that—*he and Erelah were fucking.* "By the time we were finished, everyone was gone. I still haven't had a chance to contact my brothers and find out what went down." And he was hoping like hell they were still alive and not being roasted for dinner by Elyon's dark Regiment.

"Tajael returned with news of your baby… and your blade." Markos nodded to the angel blade humming in Erelah's hand. "Unfortunately, the blade's short time outside the wards of your cave was enough to alert Elyon that you still lived… and thus may be carrying the child. By the time we returned with a few Guardian angelings, Elyon had already attacked your dragon contingent."

Leksander gritted his teeth. The angel spoke of this like it was just an unfortunate accident, not dragon lives at stake. "How many survived?"

"We were able to retrieve most of your warriors and both of your brothers," Markos said, coolly.

Relief gushed through Leksander. Erelah squeezed his hand and smiled her relief. "Where are they now?" he asked Markos. If the angel brought them here…

"My Guardian angelings were able to transport them back to your keep, out of harm's way, but we couldn't force Elyon's Regiment from the cave—their numbers were too great. By the time we returned here to gather reinforcements and send the call out to other angels of the light to garner their help… Razael had already fought off Elyon and taken hold of Erelah and the baby."

That wasn't exactly how it went down between Razael and Elyon, but Leksander wasn't going to fill him in.

Erelah did it instead. "My father promised Elyon he would turn me to shadow. The last thing Elyon wants is for me to be here, in the light."

"As long as he doesn't know, we should be fine… right?" Leksander asked.

Tajael gestured to the blade in Erelah's hand. "Normally, Elyon would know you by your blade. But he witnessed your separation from it, with you being sequestered in the cave while the blade was with the forces of the light. He will assume that is still the case and you are with your father. But he will not be fooled for long."

Markos stepped closer to Erelah. He held a hand out in blessing over her belly, which was still flat, without actually touching her. The baby was less than a day old, and already the world was coming unhinged over it. "Your child's magical signature will grow with it. This is an angeling of light. Elyon will be drawn to it and eventually realize what has happened." He gestured her forward, out of Leksander's arms. "Come, let me bless this child who will change angelkind forever."

Leksander restrained the growl welling up inside him as Erelah hurried forward to let Markos lay a hand on her belly. When he did, her back arched, and she let out a little gasp as the angel pulsed his power into her. Leksander *knew* it wasn't sex, but his wyvern form was surging under his skin, wild with jealousy. It seemed to go on forever, and Erelah was too fucking blissful when it was done. Leksander gathered her back into his arms when it was over.

"Thank you," Erelah whispered, her words definitely for Markos and not him.

"You and the child will be safe in my Dominion," he said. "You may return to your cell now."

Erelah was nodding, but Leksander gave him a pinched look. He did *not* like this idea that somehow Markos was in charge, saying when they could go and where.

Markos faced to him. "We can prepare you a cell as well, prince of the House of Smoke."

What? Fuck no. "I'll be sleeping with Erelah."

Tajael cringed, but Markos didn't seem perturbed by the anger in Leksander's voice. "As you wish," Markos said then turned and strode from the room.

"Is there anything I can get you?" Tajael asked, still looking uncomfortable.

What the hell? Did they *expect* them to sleep in separate quarters? "No, we're fine." Leksander didn't loathe Tajael as he did Markos—the angeling had done nothing but help —but he'd had his fill of "help" from angelkind for the moment.

"I'll need food. Eventually. Not just yet," Erelah said, her voice still a little blurry from the blessing from Markos.

Leksander grimaced. He should have thought of that. "Just bring it to Erelah's cell when you have a chance," he said to Tajael. Then he found Erelah's hand with his and gave her a look that said, *Can we please get the fuck away from these people now?*

She nodded, but when she led him from the training room, it was with light and slow steps, as if she were float- ing. Leksander's need to have her—to *pleasure* her in a way that would compete with this bliss-feeling she got from Markos—just grew as they wound through the brightly-lit crystal-walled hallways.

When they finally arrived at her room, he couldn't wait to close the door.

It was just as stark as he remembered—no furniture or artwork, only a perch high overhead in the narrow room— but he'd forgotten how small the bed was. It was just meant for one, and it wasn't like angelings slept all that much.

But that was okay—he didn't intend on sleeping much either.

Erelah drifted to a wall, pressed it gently to open a secret drawer, then placed her shiny-new Markos-blessed angel blade inside. Leksander was glad to see it go, and he was ready to see her tightly-wrapped angel toga leave as well.

He came up behind her as soon as the drawer was

closed and slipped his hands around her to cup her breasts. "I've been dying to touch you," he whispered into her hair, leaning in and pressing her gently against the wall. His cock got the memo and was rising to the occasion. But Erelah seemed not to—she twisted in his arms to face him, leaving his hands with nothing but wall to hold.

She peered up into his eyes. "You need to make love to me, Leksander."

"Hell yeah, I do." He bent to kiss her, hands in her hair, pressing her back against the wall. He was so absorbed in the kiss, plundering her mouth with his tongue, *claiming* her once again with his body… he almost missed that she wasn't as enthusiastic about this as he was. He pulled back, breathless, his now-rock-hard erection sandwiched between them. "What's wrong?'

She seemed to struggle for words. Then she dropped her gaze to his chest. They were still clothed, so she toyed with the fabric there.

"Hey," he said, coming back to his senses a little. "Come here." He took her hands and brought her to the tiny bed. He doubted they could even lie down on it together, so he just sat and pulled her into his lap. Then he brushed the hair from her face, which was still drawn down. "What is it?"

"I'm just… worried."

"Of course, you are." God, he was such an idiot. They'd been through hell and back—literally attacked and taken to the shadow realm—and all he wanted to do was fuck. Well… that wasn't really true. He wanted to make love to the woman he loved more than life itself. But… yeah, probably looked like fucking to her.

"I'm not afraid for myself," she explained.

He smirked. "You never are. It's really inconvenient at times."

She gave him a puzzled look.

He held her tight on his lap with one arm around her back, but his other hand was free to roam. He skimmed her arm, rounded up over her breast, then trailed the backs of his fingers up her neck and to her cheek. Everywhere their bare skin met sparked magic, and he could see that working its effect on her. Lips parted. Eyes dilating. A small ripple of goose bumps along her arm. "Erelah, my gorgeous and sexy mate. You are fierce and brave and fearless. You're never afraid for yourself. It's amazing and wondrous and sexy as hell." He let his fingers trail down her neck again and started to tug at her toga, loosening its hold on her chest. He could magick it away—since he was the one who conjured it—but she needed time to decompress, relax, and enjoy the pleasure he was determined to give her.

"Your touch gives me strength," she said, a little breathy from his hand slipping into her toga and finding her breast.

Fuck, her nipples were hard, and his cock was aching. But he would take this slow and talk his way through it… to make sure she was okay.

"Good," he breathed, leaning forward to kiss her neck. "Because I'm going to touch you *a lot.*" He felt the shudder caused by his words and his touch, and it rushed a masculine pride through him. She was *his.* She carried his child. She was everything he wanted and desired and needed. And he would make damn sure the next six weeks of her life held the maximum pleasure her body could stand.

He gripped her breast, twisting her nipple, and she gave another one of those shudders. Then he pulled back and held her gaze. Her gorgeous blue eyes were already dropping to half-mast. "You may not be afraid for yourself, but you're carrying my child, princess of the House of

Smoke. And now you must allow me to pleasure and pamper and provide for you in every way possible." He gave her a mischievous smile. "For the baby."

She breathed out, a little shaky, but from pleasure, he was pretty sure. "The baby does respond, for better and worse. When we're making love, he's as quiet as a lamb. But through all the turmoil, the fighting, the shadow realm—"

He cut her off by dragging his free hand up to shush her lips. "We're free of that now. I'm no fan of Markos, but if staying in his Dominion keeps the world from interfering with this baby coming into the world, then I'll stay and make this our own personal heaven."

A small smile tugged at her lips. "Our own personal heaven."

"Damn straight." He pulled her in for a soft and lingering kiss on the lips. He loved this woman—this strong, brave, amazing woman who was carrying his child—*so much.* His heart ached with the love he had for her, and it trembled in awe of the love he would feel for this tiny baby, who was barely more than a thought so far.

But someday… someday, he would hold his infant son in his arms.

He finished the kiss before he choked up, then he slipped his hand into her hair, fisting it and tilting back her head, so her neck was open to him. He nipped at the delicious magic of her skin, tasting her and reveling in the small moan that vibrated in her chest.

"How shall I take you, angeling of light?" he whispered hoarsely into her skin. "Because I *will* have you. *Now.*"

She whimpered, and that went straight to his cock. She said something, but it was just a breath.

"Louder, my sexy hot angeling." He bit down on her

neck because he really couldn't stand it much longer. He needed to be buried in her.

"From behind," she gasped out.

Oh, really? He released her hair and grasped hold of her waist, lifting her off his lap and standing her on her own two legs.

"From behind it is," he said, rising up himself. He turned her to face the wall opposite the bed, which really wasn't far away—just a few feet. This cell of hers was more of a monk's retreat than a bedchamber… but he planned to christen every square inch.

"Hands up," he commanded, taking hold of her wrists and planting her palms flat on the wall. He pressed his chest against her back, forcing her against the wall and nudging her legs apart with his knee. He held one of her hands in place above and used the other to run a rough, groping feel up the length of her body. She was already breathing hard. "I'm going to fuck you so hard, angel girl," he whispered in her ear.

He magicked away their clothes, making her gasp at the sudden skin contact. His cock was blessedly free now, but it was pressed into her delicious bottom… not quite where he wanted to be yet. He slid lower, still pressed against her, and the small moan that elicited made his heart rush. *Fuck,* he wanted her so badly. He slid his hand between her legs and decided to not waste any more time.

He held her one hand pinned to the wall and reached around with the other to find her sweet spot. She gasped again when he flicked the nub of pleasure that made his angel sing. Then he lifted her slightly away from the wall, just enough to position his cock at her entrance.

"You are mine, angel girl," he growled as he thrust into her.

She cried out, and *fuck…* she was so tight. Every single

time. He didn't know what magic made that work, but no matter how often he took her, it was always like he was deflowering her for the first time. He groaned, pulled back, and thrust up hard. Again and again. He picked up speed when she started clawing at the wall, crying out with each thrust. Then he had to hold her down, his hand pressing her shoulder to the wall, just because his thrusts into her hot tightness were making her move entirely too much. Then suddenly, he could feel it—the delicate quivering that presaged her coming—and he braced for that even as he kept thrusting.

"Leksander! Yes. Oh, God, *yes.*" Then her words dissolved into whimpered cries... and then the angelsong hit. The sound ricocheted around the small room, battering them both as her body convulsed, grabbing at his cock and milking it as she came.

Oh, fuck. But he held off, keeping his own climax at bay as he kept pumping into her. When she'd crested the wave of pleasure, and her song dimmed, he slowed and pulled her away from the wall. Gripping her shoulders with both hands, he swung her towards the bed. He was still buried deep inside her, and it only took a step to get her bending over, hands flat on the thin pad of her mattress. In this position, he could really grab hold and let his wild side loose.

He caressed her pert little bottom. "I have to say... I very much like this view."

She was still breathing raggedly, the sweet flesh of her sex all inflamed from coming once. The trick would be getting her there again before he lost it. He gripped her hips and drew back to slam into her. She cried out his name and nearly tumbled over with the force of it.

"You all right there, love?" He stayed buried until he got a response, just a whimper, but it was enough. He started slow, pumping in and out, but that didn't last long. Soon he was jack-hammering into her, driving the tight-coiling need low in his belly tighter and tighter. Her soft cries and calling of his name spurred him on. They rocked the bed with the violence of it until she was all the way up on the mattress, knees digging in, hands braced against the wall, toes curling in the air as she cried out.

Finally, he felt it coming—his balls tucking up hard, an eruption about to blow. He kept pounding through it, holding her against his insistent slams, but when it hit, he nearly doubled over, sinking in and welling up a deep and guttural growl. *Possessive.* Instinctual. It wasn't his wyvern, but it was damn close.

She brought out the beast in him.

He came and came, emptying everything he was into her. And then the exhaustion swept up and grabbed hold of him, dragging him down. He brought her with him as he collapsed on the small mat that somehow would serve as their bed for the next six weeks. He would have to conjure something more comfortable, but right now, he just curled around her, touching her everywhere, holding her close.

She murmured into his chest and nuzzled into him. Then she sighed the deep sigh of complete sexual satisfaction. At least, that's what he hoped that was. Her limbs were heavy, her eyes closed, and for angelings who never needed rest... she seemed halfway to unconsciousness already.

He kissed her gently on the cheek, closed his eyes, and let sleep take him.

Chapter Seven

"I do not think this is wise," Erelah said.

Leksander was leading her through Markos's Dominion. Neither time nor day mattered truly in the angel realm, and there always was someone in the halls or the gathering room or the training room. They would be spotted.

"If I had to stay in that tiny cell of yours one more minute…" Leksander gave her a devilish backward glance as he led her along the glowing crystal-walled hallways. "I'd have strung you up to the ceiling again."

"I can think of worse fates." She smirked.

He chuckled quietly but didn't slow down. So far, they'd only encountered one angeling on his way to the training room, but Devos had stopped cold in the hallway to stare. Of course, word had gotten around that Erelah and her mate were here. They'd been making love in her cell for over a week, and the entire Dominion could hear her moans and cries and angelsong if nothing else. Normally, if one heard moaning in Markos's realm, it was a fair guess that someone was serving time in one of the Penance rooms. When she had shown one of the smaller ones to Leksander—just a quartet of stations—he'd been very… aroused. Ever since, even though she said he could conjure whatever restraints he wished in her cell, he'd been after her to return to the rooms themselves. For decidedly *non*-Penance purposes.

She'd finally agreed if only to offer some diversion.

She absently patted her belly. It was slightly rounded now, and her child grew stronger every day. She could feel his angel power increasing, which both swelled her with Pride and planted seeds of worry in her mind. Markos was right that with the baby's strength would come the ability for Elyon to sense him. Perhaps. She didn't understand how well the angel might discern an infant angeling amongst a Dominion full of them. Normally, when an angel or angeling Fell and produced a child, the mother remained somewhere in the mortal world—until either the shadow or light forces showed up to claim the child, the mother, or both.

She had already been claimed.

But she was no ordinary mortal woman seduced by angel power. She and her baby were the beginning of a new day for angelkind. As the days and hours passed, she felt more and more strongly that this *must* be Righteous—if not, how could it be? Her True Love for Leksander made all their Lustful lovemaking no longer a Sin. They'd been making love for a week while inside Markos's Dominion! Such a thing was unprecedented. That dangerous surge of Pride kept rearing up each time she gave herself over with abandon to Leksander and all his pleasure-taking and receiving—and yet she remained in the light. Her wings proved it every day, and each day, her Pride surged a little more.

Would *that* be her downfall? And then, what of the baby?

As Leksander led her down one turn after another—he had quickly figured out the tangled layout of Markos's domain—she tried to imagine what the Dominion would be like if all angelings of the light mastered this skill as she had. This ability to keep the darkness at bay, seemingly without effort, while enjoying every position and pleasure Leksander had to offer.

It would be an orgy like the angel realm had never seen.

Except in shadow.

This made her frown even as Leksander pulled her to a stop in front of a door. He waved it open and stood on the threshold with her at his back.

"Fuck me," he whispered, in awe of the contents of the Penance room.

She edged past him and gave the half-smile he seemed to love. "I think that's my job." Then she sauntered into the room and took a fresh look at the equipment she would only have considered for pain before.

There was the stock, wooden clamps meant to hold an angeling's wrists while she knelt and considered her Sins. Also hooks in the ceiling meant for tying and hanging—the kind of immobilization that Leksander had played with before, but here was meant to remind an angeling of his Humility. Then there was the whipping wall, something rarely used, and only because an angeling's guilt was threatening to pull them down into shadow. A flogging released the guilt, and the wounds were quickly healed, given an angeling's immortal nature. The pain was a *release.* But that was definitely *not* something that interested her for use with Leksander... although she suspected he might enjoy it. It would pain her too much, and not that edgy pain/pleasure that often tipped her into orgasm—she simply could not administer his "punishment." Finally, there was a cage for confinement, too small for standing much less wing expansion, and once again meant for Humility training. But the pleasure potential of that would be limited.

She turned to face Leksander.

He was still standing by the door, though it was now closed. His eyes were glazed with some imagined pleasure. She would definitely fulfill whatever fantasies he had for her in this room. But first, it was long overdue for *him* to take a turn in these games.

"Conjure me a rope," she said with a smile. She held out a hand to beckon him further into the room.

His eyes took on a hungry cast. He lurched forward and fell to one knee, a long length of rope appearing in his outstretched hands. "My lady."

She took it and smirked. "Now, up against the wall." She waved her fingers at the whipping wall with its shackles made of iron, two for the wrists and two for the ankles, spread wide. She would bind him tightly, but since he conjured the rope, he could easily release himself. Not that Leksander would do such a thing, no matter how much she tormented him.

She knew his Pride would not allow it.

He hustled over to the wall and stood against it, arms and legs spread. She had to suppress a laugh—he was *facing* the wall. "This is not a flogging, my love."

He turned around, almost looking disappointed.

She grinned. "Not that kind, anyway." She magicked away her clothes and unfurled her wings, letting the rope drop and drag as she approached him. *"Hands up,"* she commanded, lifting her voice to just below angelsong.

He jolted from the onslaught of sound then raised his

hands flat against the wall again. He was still wearing his clothes, but she would take care of that in a moment. First, the binding. She made an effort to not touch him except for the hand she was binding to the elevated cuff. Her expertise in knot-tying came mostly from assisting other angelings in their Penance, which was not often, but definitely required skill. A true Penitent wished to be trapped in their Penance, no hope for release until the appointed time. Thus, the knots needed to be secured with both physical strength and magic, as an angeling in agony could summon a lot of power to their aid.

For Leksander, she didn't want him wiggling free—he would have to magic his bonds away, which would be a confession of weakness she felt sure he would resist.

Once the wrist was bound, she bent to secure first one ankle with the same rope, then the next. And finally, the other wrist. Then she stood in front of him, naked, wings extended, allowing him a full view of that which he could not touch. The smile playing on his face, which he did not seem able to hide, would soon be banished.

She reached forward and seized hold of his clothes, ripping them asunder.

He gasped in surprise, then his eyes shone. "What punishment do you have in mind for me, Mistress?"

Such games he liked to play. "All the torments you have subjected me to," she said brusquely as she set about ripping the sleeves from his arms and the last shred of trousers until only tatters remained clinging where the ropes had bound him. She stood and propped her hands on her hips. "Your Penance is to suffer in kind. I may allow you to climax. I may seek my own without you. We shall see."

His grin fell from his face. "You wouldn't."

"I might." She smirked and turned around, extending

her wings to their full length. Each wingtip brushed an opposite wall, but it was more extension than she'd managed in a week cloistered in her cell, except for their brief sojourns out to tour the Dominion.

She could hear Leksander breathing heavily behind her. She flexed her wings back, letting the feathers graze his skin. Just a light brush evoked a gasp from him. Then she brought them forward and flexed them back again, this time harder. If she wished, her wings could strike a moderate blow, but she just wanted to tantalize him with the view of her naked body and the touch of her wings. Then she spun, slowly, a seductive circle which displayed her body for him while dragging the fine brush of her feathers across his skin.

His impressive erection was hard to miss.

When she stopped, her back was to him again. She walked backward, slowly swaying her hips until her back and bottom were pressed against his chest, trapping his cock between them. Then she traveled the length of his body, up and down, a seduction of touch, her body against his, no hands, just the electric magic sparking between them.

His groans were her reward.

Just when that contact seemed to please him a little too much—especially as his cock caught on the curves of her body—she stepped away. Bearing in mind how much he liked the view when taking her from behind, she bent over, giving him full visual access to her sex. She glanced over her shoulder to see him straining at his ropes, eyes hooded with lust and trained on her bottom. She reached back between her legs, pleasuring herself in a way she made sure he could see. He twitched, and the strangled sound he made was very satisfying.

Although her own hand, less so. As much torment as it

caused him, it was infinitely less satisfying than his talented fingers. She would do anything to please this man, but restraining her own need to truly have him was proving the more difficult part.

She straightened and turned, running her hands over her breasts and body the way she'd like for him to—by the way he was panting, he wanted that, too. But not yet. She wanted to bring him to that mind-blowing climax that he'd worked so hard for her to obtain. For that, she needed to discipline herself.

She stopped just inches away from his swollen cock. She grasped it hard.

"Fuck," he gasped out. Then she released him, and his strangled curse was followed by more reflexive twitching against his restraints.

Avoiding all contact with his cock, she nevertheless endeavored to touch, lick, kiss, or bite every other part of his body. Using feathers and mouth, tongue and teeth, she covered him with her love.

"Please," he begged. "Please, just… *please.*"

It surprised her how much she enjoyed that part.

But his entreaties worked a magic on her that was hard to resist. When she licked her way up from his toes for the second time, she nibbled closer to his cock, licking every inch of skin right up to the base… but leaving the rest twitching in the air. The masculine scent of him filled her senses. When he started bucking away from the wall, she held him still, hands on his hips, pressing back. His swearing took a more colorful turn.

Finally, she could resist no longer. She took his cock in her mouth, as much as she could manage, and sucked hard.

"Fuck!" Leksander cried out, followed by a delicious sort of whimpering as she worked the length of him with

her mouth and her tongue and the firm grip of her hand. She flexed her wings as she bobbed her head, working the visual for maximum effect.

She was so devoted to her task she nearly missed the popping of air and flash of light that announced the arrival of angelkind. She jerked back, releasing Leksander's cock from her mouth but remaining on her knees.

A shadow angel. *And one she knew.*

"It's true!" Micah gasped, shock riding his face. "You've stayed in the light."

Erelah recovered her senses and leaped to her feet, bracing for combat. *What was he doing here? And wielding that blade?*

He jabbed his shadow blade in her direction, but without menace. "Why don't you have your blade?" he cried out, distressed.

"I don't—"

"Doesn't matter." He dropped his gaze and shook his head like he was trying to figure something out.

"Erelah!" Leksander fell to the floor beside her, having released his own bonds. "What the hell is happening?" He seemed ready to throw himself at Micah, which would only result in bloodshed.

"Quickly!" Micah said, surging forward.

Leksander moved in front of her, but he would only get hurt that way. She blocked him with her arm. Micah reached her… *and stabbed her with his blade!*

It was just a glancing wound on her arm, but she screeched—in anger and surprise—and knocked his blade hand away. Then she pulsed power, knocking him back, but his wings unfurled, and he quickly surged toward her again.

Only now, he held the blade grip-forward, as if offering it to her. *What was he doing?*

"Take it!" he hissed. "And use it on me. Quickly!"

She grabbed the knife but then hesitated. *What in all the angels—*

"Now!" he said, looking wildly around the room.

She barely caught his meaning and lunged with a warrior cry just in time. She sailed forward, blade raised, and sunk it in his chest just as another shadow angeling popped into the room. Micah cried out—no doubt with real pain—and grappled with her, bringing her to the ground with him. She easily rolled out of his grip, leaving him wounded on the floor while she launched off the restraining cage and near wall to circle back to the second angeling. It was a female, and she was already on the attack, leading with an underhand swipe of her blade. Erelah spiraled out of the way, wings bashing against the stockade and the ceiling and the walls, crashing her to the floor. The cramped space was throwing the shadow angeling off as well. She retracted her wings and vaulted over the stockade, coming after Erelah.

"No!" Leksander leaped at the angeling, shifting midair, but he barely slowed her down.

She pulsed power to throw him back, escaping the flail of his talons and still coming after Erelah. But her beloved had delayed the angeling enough for Erelah to be ready. Just as the attack reached her, she surged up from the floor, bringing her blade in a devastating arc that sliced the shadow angeling wide open. Her angelsong ripped through the room, but she fell at Erelah's feet, gasping for air. Her body was nearly split in half—a wound she could not hope to recover from—and the convulsions were unbearable to watch. Erelah knelt and quickly severed the angeling's head, ending the torment.

It was a Mercy.

It also sickened her to the core.

Erelah dropped to her knees, clutching her stomach. The baby's power pulsed erratically. Leksander was instantly at her side. Across the room, Micah staggered to his feet, clutching the wound in his chest. She'd aimed true, missing his heart and lungs and piercing just next to his collarbone. Leksander reflexively moved in front of her, but Micah just gave her a nod and twisted away through time and space.

"What the hell?" Leksander said, his voice still filled with shock.

"Micah has saved us." Erelah grimaced and struggled up from the floor. "Someday I will owe him a multitude of lives."

Leksander scowled at the small wound Micah had inflicted on her. "What is this?" It was no doubt to make the ruse convincing while giving her time to escape.

Erelah peered at it. The inky tendrils of shadow were snaking down her arm and into her chest. A wave of dizziness swept over her. *Oh no.* "I am… it is shadow magic…" She gripped Leksander's arm. She should have foreseen this, but everything happened so fast. And Micah couldn't have known. The baby's magic pulsed, again and again. *He senses it,* she realized with horror. *He feels the shadow magic coming for him.*

"That bastard!" Leksander spat.

"No. He meant no harm." She had to hold onto Leksander now to stay upright. "The baby is…" She was breathless as the baby's magic wracked her, wave after wave. "He is fighting it." He was bigger now. Stronger than before. And he was *inside her…* where she had no defenses against his turmoil.

Leksander's arm braced her around her back, holding

her up. "We have to get out of here. They know where you are."

Erelah nodded shakily. "Micah will be forced to reveal it. We must move." The dizziness made the floor seem to lurch, but with Leksander's steady arm, she made it to the door.

Outside was no better.

Down the hall, two shadow angelings fought a single angeling of the light. They tumbled and launched off the walls and ceiling, screaming their song.

"This way," Leksander whispered, leading her away before they caught the warrior's attention. As soon as they were around the corner, out of sight, Erelah pulled him to a stop.

"*This* way," she said, taking hold of him and twisting. She wrenched them through time and space back to her cell. *It wasn't empty.* She lurched back, protecting Leksander, but then huffed relief when she saw it was only Tajael.

"Where have you *been?*" he cried out, hands thrown wide. Then he gave her the oddest look, filled with confusion and a kind of embarrassment.

She and Leksnder were still naked.

She quickly conjured clothes for both of them. "We were attacked," she said quickly. "Shadow angelings." No need to mention Micah. Besides, Tajael already knew of his help before.

"The entire Dominion is under attack!" Tajael's gaze fell on her shoulder wound and its inky shadow magic, still visible even with her conjured training toga. "Oh no."

Just then, the air popped, and Markos arrived in a blaze of light that made Erelah wince. Her baby pulsed his own magic in response, sending a wave of nausea through her. She gripped Leksander's arm once more.

"She's injured!" Leksander cried to Markos. "Do something!"

But Markos's grave look of concern mirrored what Erelah already knew. "I must fight it myself," she told Leksander. "A life kiss will only aggravate the wound. It's made of shadow."

"Fuck that," spat Leksander. "I'll heal you myself."

Before she could stop him, he'd shifted one of his fingers to talon and sliced open the palm of his hand. Markos and Tajael stood back, fascination on their faces, as Leksander pressed his hand to her shoulder wound. The jagged knife slice was small and would be easily healed if not for the shadow magic in it. Just as Leksander had done before, he used the dragon and fae magic in his blood along with the fae runes that moved along his skin—another legacy of his fae heritage—to infuse her wound with healing power. Only the inky tendrils had already worked their way to the child within her. She could feel it intertwined with him, and the battle within was unceasing. The infusion of Leksander's blood merely added to the fight, her own angel power struggling against the fae and dragon magic Leksander was giving her.

Leksander lifted his hand free, and the external wound was gone, but the internal one raged on. She gripped harder onto his arm—it was the only thing keeping her upright.

"Why isn't it working?" Leksander's face was wrought with pain.

Markos and Tajael were conferring in rapid angel-tongue. Amidst the racking surges of power of the battle within, she caught snatches. Enough to understand what they were planning.

"My blade," she whispered to Leksander. "I need it."

"You're not slaying anyone else today," he said fiercely, his eyes glassing.

Her legs gave out with the next round of power surges, and she fell halfway to her knees. "Leksander! *My blade.*"

She'd caught Tajael's attention. They'd decided.

Leksander seemed torn, but he left her on her knees, propped against the wall, and shoved past Tajael and Markos to reach the small drawer where she kept her angel blade. He brought it to her, kneeling by her side once again.

Once she had it in hand, she nodded to Tajael. "Take us."

"What?" Leksander asked, confusion writ on his face.

She would explain later. Or it would be obvious.

Tajael hurried forward and laid hands on both of them. Then he wrenched them away from Markos's Dominion.

They were going back to the keep.

Chapter Eight

Before he could blink, Leksander was on the ledge of the weigh station outside his keep.

Erelah was still in his arms, one hand clutching her blade, the other on her belly. Tajael had brought them there, to this dusty, rocky outcropping that was the holding place for any immortals wanting admittance to the keep.

"You could have just told me," Leksander complained to Tajael.

"We had to leave immediately." Tajael straightened. "Elyon's forces surprised us. Markos didn't think he would dare—"

"*Whatever.*" Leksander's focus was on Erelah. "Is the shadow magic still fighting you?" he asked her.

"It's entwined with the baby," she gasped out.

"*What?*" Leksander's eyes went wide.

"You must gain us admittance to the keep!" Tajael's voice was pitching up to panic. He was sweeping the surrounding canyon and rocky mountain above and below, probably looking for shadow angelings to pop out of nowhere.

"Right," Leksander agreed. Once they were in the keep, they could erect multiple layers of wards. That should keep out the angelings. Maybe not a dark angel like Elyon, but it wasn't like Markos's Dominion was any better protection. Apparently.

"Tajael, get us inside!" Erelah cried, cringing over her stomach.

It felt like a vise was squeezing all the air out of Leksander's chest. He looked up at Tajael. "You have to stay by her side." God, he hated leaving her. "I have to get closer to be able to drop the wards."

"And you must warn your House not to fight us." Tajael knelt by Erelah and took hold of her so Leksander could let go.

He stood up. "They won't try to fight us, Tajael." Was the angeling losing his mind?

"Markos is gathering Guardian angels as we speak. You must prepare the way for them."

Oh. "Right." He watched Erelah cringe. Her face was taking on a horrible grayish cast. "Okay." His heart was thrumming. "I'll fly toward the keep. I'll be able to drop the wards as soon as I'm about halfway there—"

"That will take too long!" Tajael reached for his arm.

Then they were twisting again, and suddenly, they were on the roof of the keep. Erelah cried out, louder this time, and slumped down on the graveled surface.

Tajael scooped her up in his arms. "I do *not* want to force her to travel again, dragon prince! Get us in!"

The keep's perimeter alarm was already blaring, a klaxon that should alert the entire keep to their presence if nothing else. Tajael had landed them close to the main conference room, so Leksander sprinted in that direction, just fifty feet away. He reached ahead and dropped the wards to the common area. A spiral door was built into the roof, and he flicked that open. Behind him, Tajael was flying with Erelah curled up in his arms.

"Follow me!" Leksander shouted, leaping feet first through the portal. He landed on the conference table with a thud then scrambled out of the way to make room for Tajael and Erelah. The angelings floated down through the portal, and once Tajael's snowy white wings cleared the hatchway, Leksander flicked it closed with magic and raised the wards once again.

He'd barely gotten them up before his brothers, Lucian and Leonidas, stormed the room with a half dozen dragon warriors in tow.

Leksander put his hands up. "It's all right. It's just us!"

They stumbled to a stop, but Leksander was already on the move again, taking Erelah from Tajael's arms and hurrying toward the door to the rest of the keep.

"Stay here," Lucian said to Leonidas, then he ran ahead, swiping open the door. "Are you headed to your lair?" he asked Leksander.

"Yes." *God*, he could barely breathe with the torment on Erelah's face. He tore his gaze away to make sure he didn't stumble in his headlong run through the halls. "We've got shadow angels and angelings hunting us. They stormed Markos's Dominion."

"*Holy shit*," Lucian breathed. "So double levels of wards, one around the keep and a second around your lair."

"Triple if you can find a way to do it." Leksander's voice was strained. "I'll raise the ones on the lair from the inside."

"Got it." Lucian glanced back at Tajael who was half running, half flying behind them. "What about him?"

"I'm coming with you," Tajael said to Leksander.

He didn't have time to argue. "He's fine. But there are

more on the way. Markos and Guardian angels. Let them in the keep."

"*Inside* the keep?" Lucian asked, his concern dropping a growl into his voice.

"Yes, inside!" Leksander really didn't have time for this. He finally rounded the last corner to his lair. Lucian swiped the door open, and Leksander carried Erelah through, but he needed his hands back to conjure a badass, angel-proof set of wards. The strongest he'd ever made. He couldn't set her down to make the wards because she was squirming and crying out and tearing chunks from Leksander's heart. Tajael instantly saw the problem and took Erelah from his arms.

Leksander turned back to Lucian at the door. "I'll call you. But you have to let the angels of light in, Lucian. They may be our last line of defense if the shadow angel breaks through the wards."

"Breaks *through?*" Lucian asked, wide eyed.

"Yes." Then he slammed the door in Lucian's face because he had work to do. He could hear Erelah crying out in the great room where Tajael had taken her, but Leksander had to block that out and *focus*.

He closed his eyes and reached out with his fae senses to the perimeter of his lair. *Home.* It'd been his for a hundred years, and now it would be home for his mate and his child as well. And so he put every ounce of fae magic he possessed into the wards he conjured. His normal wards were already placed, invisible inkings painted during the construction of the building itself. They were easy enough to raise and lower, given he crafted them and left them ready for just the final completion spell. But *this...* this was different. He infused those ancient symbols with his even more ancient fae magic. He bound them with his True Love for Erelah, buttressing them with a pledge that if they were broken, he would forfeit his life. He emptied himself of magic, pouring it all into protection for his mate. *His child.* It was an ancient magic, born of love and promised death.

A similar magic forged the fabric of the ten-thousand-year-old treaty that ruled the House of Smoke. A fae queen of the Summer Court had vowed protection over her dragon lover and their child, casting a spell that was sealed by her death at the hands of her enraged and jealous husband. That queen's blood ran through Leksander's veins, and *he* among the three brothers had always carried more of that fae magic—as if the triplets in their mother's womb had only so much to go between them, and Leksander won the larger share.

Now he would use it to make sure the House of Smoke endured.

Placing the spell went quickly but sapped him completely. He slumped against the wall of his entrance-way, laboring over every breath. He was lightheaded, but it was done. He could raise or lower it just like the normal wards before, but the creation of it had taxed him almost to exhaustion. He was so drained, it took him a moment to piece together the words he heard drifting in from the great room.

"Erelah, no!"

"You must *help* me, Tajael!"

Holy angels of light… what was happening now? He lurched further into his lair. Then he nearly stumbled over his own feet when he saw what was happening. Erelah was propped up at one end of the couch in the center of the great room holding her angel blade poised above her belly! Tajael was holding it as well, but as Leksander rushed to the couch, he saw that Tajael was trying to wrestle it *away* from Erelah whereas she was trying to plunge it into her own abdomen.

"Erelah, what are you *doing?*" he gasped, coming around the couch but hesitating. He didn't want to jar this war of angeling strength—he might accidentally hurt her.

That distraction was enough to break Erelah's concentration, and Tajael was able to wrest the blade away. Or maybe it was something happening with the baby because she immediately curled up over her slightly-rounded belly again.

Leksander fell to his knees by her side. "My love, what can I do?"

She was panting, and the grayish cast to her cheeks was even worse—almost as if the inky shadow magic had spread and intensified. Was that even possible? The only other explanation would be that his mate was dying before his eyes, and he refused to even entertain that idea.

"Leksander," she panted through gritted teeth. Her eyes were closed. "Listen."

"I'm listening, my love." He placed his hand over hers, which was clutching her belly.

She drew in two deep breaths before trying to go on. "The shadow has reached the baby. The baby is strong... he is *fighting*... but he cannot win."

"I can try infusing more healing magic." He slid his hand to her belly and focused so his runes would race to his hand. But he'd just used every ounce of magic to conjure the wards. It would regenerate given time, and he might have some left, but it was mostly just his less-powerful dragon magic.

"*My blade.*" She was curling up again, grimacing.

"You can't... I can't let you hurt the baby, Erelah. There has to be another way." *God, his heart.* She was killing him with this.

"Not *hurt...*" She panted. *"Help."*

Leksander looked to Tajael standing over them. He was holding Erelah's blade limp in his hand and looking horrified.

Tajael blinked. Twice. "She means..." He swallowed then dragged his gaze from Erelah's tormented face to look Leksander in the eyes. "She means to destroy the shadow influence with her blade. I don't..." He just shook his head, helplessly. "I can't imagine how this can succeed."

"Leksander!" Erelah gasped.

"My love?" He felt like his heart was tearing in two.

She pried open her eyes to squint at him. *"Trust... me."*

And he did. Absolutely. This angeling he loved, who would risk anything and everything for him, and now for their baby... there was no way she would do something that would harm the child. No way she would attempt something she might not survive. Because she had to live for the baby to live, and that was everything now.

"Okay." Leksander nodded, then turned to Tajael and held out his hand for the blade.

The angeling still wore horror on his face, but he turned it over, handle first. Leksander held the blade out to Erelah. His heart was shaking so badly he was surprised to see his hand still steady.

Erelah grasped it in one hand then splayed her other one over her belly. She placed the tip of the blade between her finger and thumb but didn't press in. Then she lay her head back on the arm of the couch and closed her eyes.

She took several panting breaths and then said, "Tajael. Hold me. I must not move."

Tajael jolted as if shocked, but he braced his hands against Erelah's shoulders, holding her to the couch.

"Leksander." Her breaths were coming shorter and shorter. "My legs."

He was so choked up, he couldn't respond—he just moved on top of her legs, pinning them to the couch and bracing both hands on her hips. He didn't have Tajael's angel strength, but he would do what he could.

"Okay," she whispered, softly, to herself. "It's okay." Or possibly to the baby. "It's all right, little one. Hold still." Then her teeth clenched as the blade slowly sunk into her belly. Leksander felt her body jolt with the pain, again and again. Blood welled and flowed, spreading wide and fast along her snow-white toga. Leksander had to bite down on his own tongue to keep from crying out, distracting her, doing anything but holding her still, precisely as she asked. A keening sound came from deep inside her chest, and when tears ran down her face, they crested and fell from Leksander's too. "Aaahh... aaahhgh..." Her cries broke loose, and her body jerked against his hold. Leksander leaned in, his tears dripping down, their healing power bringing a tiny measure to the bloodbath coating his beloved's body. Then she started panting instead of crying, and Leksander feared the worst. That whatever she was trying, she would fail. Whatever grace or luck or joy he'd had until now would slip away with one cut of this blade. "Aah!" she cried out suddenly, jolting him, but then she yanked the blade up and free of her body. Her arm fell loose by her side, and the blade fell from her hand to the carpet below.

Her body went limp.

"Erelah!" Leksander cried out, climbing off her legs and reaching for her face. It was slack, spent, grayish in color... but she was still breathing. Leksander jerked his head up to face Tajael. "Heal her!"

The angeling was staring at her bloody abdomen. "It's gone."

Leksander's heart seized. "The baby?"

Tajael whipped his gaze to Leksander's. "No! The shadow." Then he bent down and breathed into Erelah's gaping open mouth, giving her a life kiss. Leksander leaned away then reached for her belly, covering it with both hands. Her blood was hot on his palms, but he channeled what little magic he had, bending over her to add his tears, praying and praying that it was enough. That the baby would make it. That between the two of them—him and Tajael—they could keep her from dying as she saved their child.

He could feel Tajael's angel magic flooding her system, sealing the wound below his palms. The bleeding stopped. Leksander reached out with his fae senses to the child within… and the baby's essence still burned bright. Fae and dragon and angeling combined. This child was truly a miracle.

Erelah pulled in a deep breath, and when Leksander looked, Tajael had pulled away. He looked drained—cheeks hollowed and darkness under his eyes—but a smile was on his face.

Tajael gave him a nod just as Erelah breathed out and opened her eyes.

"My love." Leksander wiped the blood from his hands and found hers so he could hold them. She squeezed back and tilted her head enough to smile at him. The relief was so intense, Leksander almost collapsed. He leaned against the couch and managed to stay upright. *"Holy magic,* woman. You almost scared the life out of me."

She let her head fall back, but the smile remained. "You're not allowed to die yet, dragon prince. I'm not finished with you."

He huffed a strangled laugh and grinned and then just shook his head.

She tilted her head back further. "You gave too much," she said to Tajael.

"I would have given more had you needed it," he said with a gentle smile.

Any other time in his life, Leksander would have felt a burning jealousy with the smiles they were exchanging. Now, he felt nothing but gratitude. And relief. And an inarticulate joy.

They were safe—at least, as safe as they could be.

Erelah was alive. The baby lived.

All was going to be well.

Erelah picked up her head and frowned at him. "I think I have need of food." She seemed perplexed by this, but Leksander couldn't have loved those words any more.

He laughed. "Your wish is my command, princess of the House of Smoke."

Chapter Nine

"Just for a moment," Erelah pleaded. "What harm can come of it?"

"No." Leksander kissed her on the forehead then scooted down the couch to kiss her belly. She was two weeks into the pregnancy, and it had become very noticeable. "You can speak to him at the door."

"It would only take a second to allow Tajael inside," she reasoned. She knew Leksander could drop the wards any time he liked.

"And only a second for Elyon to find his way here." Leksander scowled and rose up from the couch where they had been cuddled after their latest round of lovemaking. He was naked, per usual, but she couldn't help admiring the way his muscular bottom flexed as he strode across the great room.

"There are three levels of wards," she tried again. "Elyon would have to break through all three at once. And in that tiny stroke of time. It's very improbable."

He stopped at a small desk on the far side of the room.

"I'm not dropping the wards," he said without looking at her, digging for something in one of the drawers.

As he strode back to her, she ran a hand over her belly. The baby sang quietly in response, a tiny angelsong that spoke of his contentment. Leksander had kept her in a state of bliss all week, ever since she recovered from the self-performed surgery that was necessary to excise the shadow from her baby. She had to stop it before it could fuse with the child… or it would kill the baby in the trying.

She knew of the dangers of dropping the wards. She simply judged them to be low. Whereas Leksander was unwilling to take any risk, no matter how small.

He tossed her the phone he had apparently retrieved from the desk. He had called his brothers intermittently over the last week—even used the screen in his bedroom for live video conversations—all so they could keep him apprised of the developments in the keep, including that Markos had bunked a small legion of Guardian angels in amongst the dragons. Which was precisely what Erelah wanted to talk to Tajael about.

Leksander gestured to the phone. "You can call Leonidas. He'll track down Tajael and get him over here. You can talk at the door for whatever you need." Then he kneeled on the couch and kissed her toes, her ankles, her shins… "Or you could simply let me distract you until you forget all about the world outside my lair."

She pulled up her legs, away from his tempting touch. "I know Tajael. He would keep any concerns from me that he judged I didn't need to know… unless I press him."

Leksander sat back, mild approval on his face. "Tajael is a wiser angeling than I knew."

"He is stubborn and occasionally untruthful. Just like you," she teased.

He gave a look of offense. "When have I been untruthful?"

She rose up from the couch, phone clutched in her hand, then bent to kiss him briefly on the nose. "Only the decades-long silence in which you did not profess your love for me."

He scowled. "Other than that." Then he tried to capture her around the waist, but she danced back out of his reach.

She braced her hands on her hips, standing naked before him. "Are there any other untruths you wish to confess at this time?"

His face blanched. "Um… no?" But she could see the calculation on his face.

Which only made her laugh—softly, so he wouldn't take offense. Then she conjured a training toga so she would be dressed to meet Tajael—and less of a temptation for her mate—and sauntered forward to climb onto his lap on the couch. She straddled him, and his eyes lit up with interest. If she were still naked, she felt sure they would be joined before she could get a word out. Even the toga was still amenable to that purpose.

"Your soul is pure and righteous, dragon prince of the House of Smoke," she proclaimed. Then she kissed him briefly. "Whatever small thing you think you may have hidden from me matters not next to the shining of your heart."

He gazed up at her and gripped her hips to bring her closer. "You can see it, can't you? My soul."

"Yes." And she could. All angelings were gifted with that discernment from their angel side. It was what made humanity so alluring, the bright goodness of their souls. And dragons as well, at least the righteous ones of the

House of Smoke. "You are good to the core, dragon prince. I've loved you from the beginning for it."

He growled and slipped his hand under her shirt. "Show me your love, angel girl."

She chuckled. They had been doing nothing but showing their love for the endless hours of the last week. She scooted back off his lap, working free of his grasp. He did not readily let her go—his erection was standing proud, and they had just finished minutes ago. "You will not die if we wait a short spell," she said.

"Don't be so sure!" he called after her as she crossed the room.

She laughed again as she lightly ascended the stairs, heading for the bedroom and a shower. Her angel nature —the one that allowed her little sleep and less food— normally meant she had little need for showering as well. But endless lovemaking brought out her human side all too thoroughly, and she wanted to refresh before meeting Tajael at the door.

She quickly texted Leksander's brother, Leonidas, and asked him to arrange for Tajael to come to the door of the lair so they could speak. Then she stepped into the expansive shower that Leksander had just off his bedroom. She magicked away her clothes, and as the warm water tumbled over her skin, she remembered the first time her body had been awakened to these pleasures that Leksander brought out of her. Here, in his shower, she had learned she could pleasure herself as well. What an enlightenment! Back then she still lived in fear of turning shadow, but if there were anything the last two weeks of being mated to Leksander had proven, it was that Lust would not be her downfall. Not a second time. Love had rescued her.

But that didn't mean she was immune to all the Sins.

Pride was the one she felt bubbling deep within her,

growing stronger each day as her child grew. Pride that she among angelings would be the one to bear him. That she could dip into the forbidden ecstasies of love and remain in the light. The fate of the two realms—mortal and immortal—rested on her ability to deliver this child to Leksander, and she had already rescued the baby from shadow with her own blade! Surely, angelings would sing of her for centuries to come. Surely, others would be tempted to follow her path.

And *that...* that was the danger she saw. The reason she needed to speak to Tajael. To take the true measure of the impact of this miraculous pregnancy. And perhaps garner his help in restoring her Humility because she feared if it kept slipping away... she might find herself Falling before she realized what was happening.

The water was cool and wonderful on her heated skin. The longer she carried the child, the stronger he became, the more the fiery heat of angel and dragon burned inside her. The shower was wet and sensual, but the endless love-making left her with no desire to pleasure herself. She finished the shower, magicked the water away, and returned to a properly clothed state. Although, even now, she was painfully aware of how *bare* the standard angeling toga was—two strips that covered her breasts, a golden chain between them, and a short skirt draped over her hips. Leksander had requested more than once that she wear it while he was taking her, so she was very aware of the possibilities it posed. But Tajael knew nothing of this— he was innocent of the kind of sexual awakening she'd experienced.

At least, she assumed that was true.

He had been in shadow for a time, so anything was possible.

But more on point was the status of the rest of the

angelings of Markos's Dominion. And on *that*, Tajael should have a keen insight. One she hoped to gain.

By the time she returned downstairs, Leksander was snoring on the couch.

She had to physically cover her mouth to stifle her laugh. He insisted so fervently on their lovemaking, she forgot he still needed rest. And it was well that he would get some now, while she conferred with Tajael. She didn't want Leksander to worry about her worries.

The front door of the lair was around the corner and down the short entranceway—far enough that if their voices were kept low, they shouldn't wake Leksander. When she reached it, Tajael was already there.

"Erelah!" he exclaimed, straightening up from where he leaned on the doorframe. "Are you well?" His gaze bounced up and down her body, lingering on her belly, which protruded through the skimpy wrappings of her toga.

"I am well. And the baby, too." She smiled and fluttered light finger-taps on her belly. The baby trilled a small angelsong in response.

"He sings!" Tajael's eyes seemed ready to bulge out of their sockets.

Her smile grew, and she felt that dangerous *Pride* surge again. She forced herself to seriousness, and remembering the need for quiet, dropped her voice. "Leksander is sleeping. Let's not wake him."

Tajael nodded fervently, his gaze still fixed on the soul of the child inside her.

"Tell me, Tajael," she said quietly. "How goes it with Markos in the keep? And his Guardians? Are the dragons accommodating? Is there trouble I should know about? Hold nothing back, or I will make you pay later."

His gaze snapped up. "The Truth, then?"

"As you know it," she insisted.

A frown settled on his face. "The impact of this baby continues to reverberate throughout the Dominion."

She nodded, encouraging him to go on.

He pressed his lips into a grimace.

"Tajael," she admonished.

"Markos hasn't said anything outright," he said. "That concerns me the most."

She leaned back. "I don't understand."

Tajael drew in a breath then dropped his gaze to his hands, which clenched one another. He wore the same toga as normal, as all angelings. If she were attracted to any man other than Leksander, she would see the appeal. Bright ice-blue eyes, earnest and intelligent. Short blond hair, as pale as his snow-white wings. The physique of quintessential human male beauty... only Tajael was unique in carrying a tattoo on his arm, a dragon, in addition to the markings of his time while in Elyon's Regiment. His toga did nothing to hide any of his masculine beauty, although she doubted he was aware of that. And while she couldn't sense it through the wards, she knew his soul shone even more beautiful and righteous. Most of all, Tajael was accomplished in the social ways of both humans and angels... and angelings who were a mixture of both. She trusted his read of the situation if only she could persuade him to share it.

"I am trapped here, Tajael," she appealed to him, gesturing to the invisible barrier of the wards between them. "Leksander shields me from all news, good or bad. He wishes me to forget the outside world even exists, but you and I both know that I cannot. *Please.* Tell me the Truth of what is happening."

Finally, he dropped his hands and held her with his

gaze. "It started back in the Dominion. Yours and Leksander's constant mating—"

"*Lovemaking,*" she interrupted him with a frown.

He tipped his head. "*Lovemaking.* It was very much noticed. And… how can I say this?" He grimaced. "Studied?"

She drew back. "How so?"

He made a face of concern. "There was much talk of what precise activities you were engaged in. How the acts were performed. What it… what it *felt like* for you and how you were able to stay in the light."

"Oh." This was far worse than she assumed. In Truth, she hadn't given much thought to it.

"Yes," Tajael agreed with her unspoken concern. "One could easily say there was a fascination about it that possessed most of the angelings and even Markos himself."

"And you?" she asked, her curiosity suddenly piqued.

He frowned. "I've spent time in shadow, Erelah. I know what orgies look like."

"Oh," she said again. He was blanking her mind with all this. "But you say Markos has said nothing about it?"

"Nothing of *concern,*" Tajael said. "He was curious at first as well, asking after you and Leksander, wishing to know what activities you were engaged in, under the guise of concern for your well-being."

"What did you tell him?" Now she was just frankly curious herself.

"That it's often difficult to tell between the dying and the orgasming?" He gave her a look like the whole thing was ridiculous. Which it was.

She giggled then covered her mouth.

Tajael scowled at her, so she worked harder to kill her smile. "But then it got worse," Tajael said, dead serious. "The attack of the shadow angelings convinced those of

Markos's Dominion that the cause of protecting you must be particularly righteous. Otherwise, why would the shadow seek to destroy you? That they almost succeeded, but you valiantly made sacrifices of pain and danger to save the child? Convinced them even more. Nearly every angeling vied to be among your Guardians, not only to be near you and Leksander and a chance to learn more about these... *activities*... but because they would be defending the House of Smoke."

"Isn't that a good thing? I mean, wishing to defend the dragons who defend humanity?" But the whole thing was sinking a dark feeling through her. Angelings of light obsessed with sex? Even as none of them had the slightest inkling of the power of Lust or how Love was required to stay in the light?

"If that were all it were, yes," Tajael said darkly. "But since they've come to the House of Smoke, they've been mingling with dragons. *Angelings and dragons,* Erelah. It's not unknown in the Dominion how sexually-driven dragons can be."

Erelah's eyes went wide. "Have any of them Fallen?" Had it already begun? Her child hadn't even been born, and already the dark forces of Vice were tempting angelkind in a way they never had before.

"No. Not yet. But Markos chose unwisely."

Erelah's eyebrows lifted. For an angeling to question the wisdom of an angel... "How so?"

"Most of the Guardians are female," he said tersely. "The dragons of the House of Smoke are male. It cannot be a mistake. I feel Markos is deliberately tempting the fates with this mingling. And I've found more than one angeling in the company of a very Lustful dragon in the less-traveled parts of the keep. It's all I can do to keep watch over them."

Erelah shook her head slowly. "I haven't even delivered the baby, Tajael."

"I know. And when you do, if both you and the baby live…" He shook his head. "The Fall could begin right here in the House of Smoke."

She blinked. "What should I do?"

Tajael gave an elaborate shrug. "This is not your problem, Erelah. Your mate is right about that. You *must* deliver this child. The treaty depends on it. I've vowed to protect you both, and I will give every last measure to that. In the meantime, I'll try to keep all of angelkind from going mad with Lust." His face twisted up in disgust.

She tried not to laugh, but there was something intrinsically funny about it. She could just see Tajael flying through the keep, hectoring the female angelings not to give into the temptations of the flesh in the form of the intensely masculine dragons roaming the keep.

Tajael started to reach out like he wanted to lay a hand on her belly, but he then jerkily pulled back, apparently just remembering the wards. "You and Leksander have wrought a miracle here on earth. You've each gone to great lengths to love one another. You've each been willing to sacrifice yourselves for the other. Your love is bright and shining and True. Hold fast to that and bring this child into the world. This folly with the dragons is just another Vice, like every other that angelings of light need to guard against. Perhaps we should institute Penance rooms here in the keep to aid them."

Once again, Erelah had to hold back her laugh. "I'm not sure that would work."

He sighed. "Regardless, it is not your concern. There, I've told you the Truth. Now worry no more and return to your mate. Let me handle what goes on outside the wards. You ensure everything goes right inside."

And in that, he made complete sense. "You are the best sort of friend, Tajael."

"I live to serve." He bowed his head, but then he gave her a small smile.

She waved him off and closed the door, hurrying back to see if they'd woke Leksander. He was still on the couch, but instead of snoring… he was growling. Face down, his body twitched, and the growling grew deeper. He was having some kind of dream, and not a pleasant one.

"Leksander!" she called out just before she knelt by his side. When he didn't respond, she touched him on the bare skin of his back. He whirled around, roaring and catching her wrist before she could yank back. But then he jerked to a stop and released her, eyes wide and roaming around the lair.

"The wards—" His eyes narrowed, then he slumped back in relief. "Still there. *Thank magic.*" He shook his head and then slid off the couch to kneel next to her where she still was on the carpet. "Did I hurt you?" A frown was carving his face.

"No, of course not." She held a hand to his face. "You dreamt the wards were down?"

He nodded then pulled her back onto the couch with him, gathering her up in his lap. He stroked her hair and her face and her belly like he was reassuring himself she was all there, her and the baby both. Then he took a deep breath and blew it out. "If those wards break, I won't be able to protect you."

"I still have my blade."

"I know." He grimaced and held her tighter. "What I mean is that I won't be here at all. I wove a death spell into them."

She leaned away. *"What?"*

"A death spell. It's when—"

"I know what it is!" She pushed off his lap and stood. A great quivering took hold of her body. "Why would you do this, Leksander?" This shaking... it took her a long moment to understand it. *Fear.* It was fear.

He looked pained. "Because the shadow angelings were attacking, we were on the run, and I had to make sure you were safe."

"But a *death* spell?" She had said she understood... but she didn't. Not really. How could he risk his life just to strengthen the wards?

He stood up and reached for her, but she backed away. "Erelah, *please.* I would give anything, including my life, for you and the baby. You know that. This is all I have to give."

"It's too much." Her voice quavered, and her body was still shaking. If anyone would be dying, it would be *her*... but not before this baby was born. If she managed that, all was supposed to be right with the world. Now she had to worry that, if they were attacked, and Elyon broke through, that Leksander would simply die.

"I'm sorry." He grimaced. "I shouldn't have told you."

This... this was the thing he was holding back when she thought there was nothing he could say that would break her True Love. And this didn't... but the idea that she might carry and bear Leksander's child but still lose him... it was making great waves of horror rock through her body.

Leksander wrapped his arms around her. "I'm sorry," he whispered into her hair. "I didn't mean to upset you."

"Take them down." It came out as a sob.

He pulled back and held her cheeks. "Not until the baby is born."

"Leksander."

"The danger is still the same." His eyes were pained,

but not enough… he would not budge on this, she could tell.

She wanted to rage at him. She wanted to be angry. But all she felt was this sense of cold terror. Because he was right—at any moment, Elyon could strike. And if he succeeded, Leksander would die. Just… die. No fight could save him. Nothing she did would matter. But he did it to protect her and the baby… and she couldn't waste any minutes being angry at him for such a selfless thing.

She leaned into him, wrapping her arms around him. "Distract me," she said. "Distract me from this."

And so he did. Starting with kisses and quickly building to more. She'd reveled in their lovemaking before, but now it seemed like a lifeline. This was how she would survive the next four weeks… buried in Leksander's arms and praying Elyon would never come.

Chapter Ten

"Hang on, let me call Leonidas," his brother Lucian said.

Leksander was conferencing with him on the screen in his bedroom. They'd taken to doing daily check-ins, which he slipped in while Erelah was resting. She did that more often now—the baby was growing, and so were her human needs for food and rest. The rest of the time, Leksander focused on pleasuring his mate and distracting her from the dangers that loomed outside the walls of his lair. She was three weeks into the pregnancy now—halfway—and he was literally counting the days to the birth. These morning calls were his way of marking time, getting through another day. Lucian's rambling reports were predictable—Markos was an asshole, the sexy female angelings were distracting his warriors, and little Larik, their father's namesake, had performed some stunning feat of dragonling prowess… like rolling over.

Leksander looked forward to it.

But bringing Leonidas into the mix was new. "How's

little Thorn doing?" Leksander asked while they waited for Leonidas.

"Good. Rosalyn and Arabella have regular playdates for the kids." Lucian seemed distracted by something off screen. When he turned back, he said, "You know they're dying to have your dragonling join the Little Prince Club."

"Tell me they're not seriously calling it that."

"Hell yeah, they are." Lucian snorted a laugh and shook his head.

Leksander made a face, but he would give anything to have life be normal in the keep once again. And with three new dragon princes? It would make all of this torment worthwhile.

He had to look away from the screen to get his emotions under control.

"Hey," Lucian said to someone off screen.

A second later, Leonidas appeared. "Hey, sorry. Had to... um... take care of a thing." He exchanged a look with Lucian that quickly turned into a wordless conversation.

The hairs on the back of Leksander's neck rose. "What's going on?"

Lucian winced but nodded to Leonidas, who spoke first, but didn't actually answer his question. "How are things with Erelah?" he asked earnestly.

"Fine." Leksander scowled. His brothers were hiding something from him... and they better knock that shit off right now. "Baby's growing. Everything's normal. She's resting and eating. Taking a nap as we speak." He waited, but Leonidas said nothing, just nodded along. "Okay, what the hell aren't you telling me?"

Now Leonidas was the one grimacing. "We wanted to make sure Erelah was out of the first trimester before we...

well, before we clued you in. Sorry, my brother. Lucian made the call."

Lucian snarled. "Sometimes, it fucking sucks to be king."

Leksander's stomach clenched. *What was happening?*

"Anyway," Leonidas continued. "The world's basically going to hell."

Lucian rolled his eyes. "Way to ease in slowly."

Leonidas put up his hands. "Hey, I thought we should have told him from the start."

"Fucking spit it out!" Leksander hissed, keeping his voice low, so he didn't wake Erelah. She was downstairs, but still. *Angelings.*

"All right, here's the deal," Leonidas said. "The demon uprising is escalating. And when I say *escalating*, I mean it's reached some kind of tipping point. Half the city is in lockdown. The humans don't know what the hell is happening, but obviously, we do. Markos has been calling on his angel friends to lend their air support, but a good fraction of his own forces are here at the keep, running patrols inside and out. It's wall-to-wall feathers here."

Leksander squinted. "How long has this been going on?"

"Pretty much since you arrived two weeks ago," Lucian replied.

"Two *weeks?*" Leksander shook his head. "With that many angelings… how do you guys *not* have this under control?"

Lucian cringed, but it was Leonidas who answered. "It turns out those angel assholes of the light? They don't have anywhere near as many angelings as the shadow ones."

Leksander frowned. "The shadow angelings are in Seattle?"

"They fucking *own* Seattle," Leonidas said.

"That's not true," Lucian grumbled.

"Close enough." Leonidas scowled at him then turned to face the screen. "Basically, it's angeling war over the city while the demons are running amok. We're losing angelings every day."

"Holy shit," Leksander said, the impact of this finally hitting him. "But why? I mean... the demon thing is Zephan's doing. Why would the shadow forces... oh. Shit."

"Yeah." Leonidas nodded. "Zephan's in league with the shadow angels and angelings. Or at least this one guy, Elyon, and his troops."

Leksander rubbed a hand across his face. This was fucking *bad*. "Erelah said Elyon was supposed to turn her over to the fae. Which, I'm sure, was Zephan. But Elyon's got his own issues with the angels of the light. Are we sure this is the fae's doing?"

"At a minimum, Zephan set all this in motion," Lucian said. "He's the one who enhanced the vampires to infect the humans with demon essence. Hard to say if it's escalating now because he did something *more...* or if it's just now coming to a head. Either way, it's hell out there right now for humanity."

"I think this is 100% Zephan," Leonidas said. "The hacking attacks... that's got to be him."

"Wait, what?" Leksander said. "What hacking attacks?"

"The first wave was on our security systems," Lucian said. "But the fae know fuck-all about computers. That could have just been—"

"That was *not* a coincidence," Leonidas cut him off. "And Zephan *pretends* to be clueless about lowly human technology, but the boy developed magic-spliced gene-tech for vampires. He has a fucking clue."

Sweet magic. "Did Zephan breach our security?" Leksander asked, his voice hiking up.

"We've cut off access to the outside world," Lucian said. "Went old school with patrols and lookouts. Dragons and telepathy. He won't catch us by surprise if that's what he's thinking."

"But the wards…" Leksander's mouth was running dry. "They're still up, right?" He could tell nothing —*obviously* —from inside his lair, not with his own personal wards up.

"Still up," Leonidas confirmed. "But there have been concentrated magical attacks on those too. Sporadic. Different kinds. He's fucking pounding on the door, Leksander. Not to alarm you, but it's really a situation out here."

Leksander scrubbed a hand over his face. *"Holy shit,* we've got three more weeks to go."

"We'll hold them off," Leonidas said with a *lot* more confidence in his voice than Leksander was feeling at the moment. "But you've got to get that baby born. Once that happens, Zephan's got no quarrel with the House of Smoke anymore. The treaty renews; he stops fucking with us. And the rest of humanity. It's that simple. And I'm pretty sure that's the only solution at this point because we're not winning this on dragon power. Or even angel power. We're in a siege. Holding tight, but still. This is a war of endurance. We'll hold the line, my brother, but get that baby born."

"Right." Leksander swallowed. "Okay. I'm not telling Erelah *any* of this. None of it, you understand?"

Lucian raised his hands, gesturing to the screen and giving Leonidas a look that said, *See? I told you.*

Leonidas scowled in return. "Tell him," he said to Lucian.

"There's fucking *more?"* Leksander's voice screeched a

little, and he fought to keep it down. He really didn't want to wake Erelah.

Lucian grimaced but turned to face him. "Tajael's gone missing. We're pretty sure the shadow have him."

"Ah, *fuck.*" Leksander cringed, actually stepping back. "Okay, that *cannot* get to Erelah's ears. Not before the baby comes."

"Agreed," Leonidas said.

"And you'll let me know if the wards are breached." Leksander put a warning in his voice.

"Absolutely," Lucian said with a nod for emphasis.

"And there's one more thing," Leksander said, wincing at the slightly-alarmed look on his brother's faces. "I wove a death spell into the wards around my lair. If they go down… you'll have to come in and defend Erelah and the baby for me." He should have told them this two weeks ago, but he had no idea things were so dire.

"You did *what?*" Lucian threw out his hands then jammed them into his hair like he would pull it out.

"Erelah knows," Leksander added. "Just get your asses in here and save them, okay?"

"You know we will," Leonidas said. Lucian was still cursing under his breath.

Leksander nodded. "I've got to go. She could wake any time now. These angelings don't sleep much."

"Yeah, tell me about it." Leonidas rubbed the back of his neck.

That's when Leksander noticed the dark circles under both his brothers' eyes. They must have been running ragged, keeping the crazed world away from him and his mate and his child.

Leksander pressed a hand to the screen. "Thank you, my brothers."

Leonidas put his palm to the screen. Lucian grumbled under his breath but did the same.

Leksander reached out to magically swipe the screen off. Then he let out a deep sigh. Somehow he had to wipe all this from his mind and keep Erelah blissfully unaware as long as possible.

Three weeks.

It was an eternity.

And it felt like Erelah's End of Times was already happening, right outside their walls. Which was precisely why she couldn't know anything about it. Zephan's attacks —and he was sure Leonidas was right, this was all Zephan, even if Elyon was doing his ugly bidding—were all about making sure Erelah didn't deliver their child. The best way —possibly the *only* way—to defeat him would be to surround Erelah in a blanket of love and protection and bliss until their son took his first breath.

Then fuck that fae. Leksander would find a way to kill him.

For now, everything was about Erelah.

He scrubbed his face once more, took a deep breath, plastered his most winning smile on his face, and strode from his bedroom to seek his mate.

Chapter Eleven

Two more weeks.

Erelah only had two more weeks to carry this child, but her belly was already enormous. She sat propped at the head of Leksander's bed, and she could barely see her legs folded underneath her. She remembered when Arabella and especially Rosalyn had carried their dragonlings. She was present at the birthing, helping each in that time of magical need. She did not recall their bellies swelling so large. Or their breasts. Or that the raging need for sexual pleasure was both more intense and more satisfying.

They would not have shared that last part.

"Are you done?" Leksander asked, clearing away the wrappings for several flavors of cheese, an entire sleeve of crackers, now empty, and a bowl that once held grapes.

She swallowed down the last bite. "I didn't think it was possible to eat this much."

Her mate grinned as he carried off the detritus of her second meal of the day. Perhaps her belly was as large as it was because of the food she was consuming. On the other hand, the baby hummed his delight as the sustenance hit her bloodstream and fed him as well. She drummed her fingers on her belly, and the baby kicked a small foot out with impressive strength for one so small. He would make a good warrior someday.

Leksander returned as she played this secret game with his son—tapping one part, getting a response, then tapping another. She'd conjured a toga for her mealtime, but the bare skin of her belly stretched far beyond the confines of the cloth.

Leksander settled on the bed next to her. "What are you doing?" he asked, eyes alight.

"Give me your hand," she instructed.

He gave her a curious look but complied. She placed it on her belly so he would feel the tiny kicks when they came.

"Now spread your fingers like this." She splayed her hand on the opposite side.

He did so. "I don't need instructions in how to touch you, Erelah." He was giving her that sexy look that said he was ready to make love again.

She gave him a pretend scowl. "Now, between your fingers, tap like this." She showed him, and when he repeated her motion, the baby punched hard right where his hand lay.

His eyes went wide. "Does that hurt?"

"No." She smiled. In Truth, it was a little uncomfortable. She could imagine this game wouldn't work so well once the baby was even larger and stronger. Which she had a hard time picturing. She *knew* Arabella and Rosalyn didn't literally explode when their child reached full term... yet it somehow felt like a possibility. This angel-dragonling might just burst his way out.

Leksander tapped twice more, the delight on his face

more than enough reward for the small pokes the baby was delivering.

Then his eyes half-closed, and he growled, "Do you have any idea how sexy you are?"

"Because my baby can perform tricks?" But she smiled. She knew he loved every part of her body as it grew with the baby—he told her in detail quite often.

"Because you are carrying my child." He kissed her belly. Then a little lower. And lower still. "And you're half naked on my bed."

"Should I magick these away and become fully naked?" she asked with a grin. Their lovemaking was virtually continuous—any time she wasn't sleeping or eating, and she had just finished both.

"No," he said as he lifted the flimsy skirt of her toga. "I like you just like this." Then he dove between her legs, his talented tongue leading the way, and soon she was gripping the white linens of his bed and calling out his name, urging him on. The largeness of her belly was forgotten in the throes of the orgasm that quickly raged up and swept through her—from her toes, which dug into the bed, to her face flushed hot with the heat of their lovemaking.

She bucked against Leksander, singing angelsong to keep from lifting him off the bed with her pulse of power, and she rode the wave until it was done. Then she slumped back into the bed. Only then did Leksander raise his head, smug masculine pride writ all over it.

"Turn over," he commanded.

And she wished to comply—especially with his cock so stiff and ready—but moving had become awkward, and her sense of being so much *larger* than normal zoomed back. Leksander quickly came to her rescue, giving her a hand up to her knees and a quick kiss on the mouth. Then he gently turned her around to face the head of the bed and the windows above it. She bent over to grasp hold of the window's edge, bracing herself as the warm afternoon sunshine streamed in. It was nothing but blue skies outside.

"Is this all right?" he murmured against her back, kissing her dragon mark and caressing her bottom. He lifted her toga skirt clear, and she felt his cock slide between her legs, but not enter her. It was a delicious feeling.

"Yes," she breathed, then she squirmed against him.

He groaned, pulled back and slowly eased into her. She gripped the window harder, but he stroked slow and deep, not the frenzied motion he used earlier in the pregnancy. He'd been exceedingly gentle with her ever since they arrived at his lair. She hinted once or twice that restraints would be more than welcome, but he would have none of it. Almost as if he thought her more breakable than before. Which was nonsense, but now with her belly so large… the slow and deep taking from behind worked her relentlessly toward her climax. And for the longer it took to get there, the more bed-shaking it would be when it arrived.

He quietly grunted, gripping her shoulder to hold her steady, but she could hear the strain in it inching higher. Her own moaning kept time with the slow beat of his thrust. Just as his breath became ragged, he slipped a hand around to the front of her sex, and his fingers quickly found her nub, sending her cresting again. It swept over her fast—too fast—somehow catching her by surprise even with the long, slow build. Her body convulsed, and her power pulsed out, launching him away before he finished.

"Leksander!" She whipped her head around.

He'd been shoved entirely off the bed, but he quickly scrambled up, returning to her and entering her once more. *Harder.* The quick, short thrusts somehow shot her higher still, but this time when the next orgasm gripped her, she shuddered and convulsed and channeled her power into angelsong. Leksander slammed into her through it, growling out his own release, his grip harder and more vigorous than normal.

Then he released her and withdrew and fell to the bed, rolling over on his back. *"Oh, fuck,"* he breathed, throwing an arm over his face and panting. "We're going to have to do that slow-fast thing again."

Her body was still reverberating with bliss. She sank into the bed next to him on her side, so as not to crush the baby.

"You can take me as hard as you like, dragon prince."

He growled and pulled his arm from his face to peer at her. "But the baby…"

The baby was humming quietly to himself. "I think he likes the rocking." She smiled.

Leksander groaned and turned on his side to face her. "Then I will *definitely* rock you." He kissed her gently on the nose. Then the lips. Then her cheek… she recognized the signs. He may be spent for the moment, but he would work another orgasm out of her before he was ready to "rock" her again.

She scooted back from his kissing.

He frowned. "What's wrong?"

"That's three orgasms by my count," she said with a smile.

He grinned. "Is there a limit?"

There should be. But between their two forms of immortal magic, there hardly seemed one in reality. "No," she admitted. "But I was thinking…"

His eyes lit up, and he propped his head on his hand. "Yes?"

"I'd like to see Rosalyn."

His face fell. "You know we can't—"

"Not in person. On the screen." She gestured toward

the giant one on the wall, the one he used for his communications with his brothers.

He frowned, but what could he possibly object to?

"We princesses of the House of Smoke have to stick together," she said with a small smile.

And she could see that soften whatever objection he had. "Okay," he said, then leaned forward to kiss her on the nose. "But Rosalyn had better not give you any terrible advice like *Stop Having Sex* or *Don't Let Leksander Nibble Your Toes,* or I'll have to have words with her mate."

"I can't imagine any dragon's mate not wanting to have sex." And it was true. She'd become almost as insatiable as Leksander since bearing his mark.

"That's because we're impossibly handsome." He leaned in to give her another kiss.

"And well versed in technique." She kissed him back.

He groaned and slipped a hand around her waist. "And we always want more." His kiss deepened.

She had to shove him away. "Perhaps she will have the cure for that." She smirked.

"God, I really hope not." He swept his gaze longingly over her body, still clothed in toga, if somewhat disheveled. "Do you want to change before I call?"

She nodded and slipped off the bed to the bathroom. She splashed her face with cool water and teased the love-mussed tangles out of her hair. Then she conjured a training toga—substantially less revealing than her standard one. Leksander's voice carried into the bathroom. It sounded like he was talking to Leonidas, Rosalyn's mate, but by the time she emerged again, only Rosalyn was on the screen.

"Here you go, love." Leksander kissed her quickly on the cheek. "I'll be downstairs." There was a lingering promise of more lovemaking in his eyes. Then he turned to leave.

She waited until he closed the door behind him. To Rosalyn, she blurted out, "How did you manage it?"

Her eyebrows hiked up, but she had a smile on her face. "All the sex? I guess I managed well enough."

Erelah couldn't help her smile. "No, I mean…" She ran her hands over the enormous mound of her belly. "This carrying of a child…" She looked up. "It's much bigger than I expected."

Rosalyn laughed. "Erelah, you're gorgeous!"

"Angelings are naturally beautiful." She frowned when Rosalyn laughed more. "It's God's gift to show his…" She trailed off because Rosalyn was gasping for air, her laughter was so strong.

"I'm sorry!" Rosalyn wiped at her eyes. "I'd forgotten you were…" She gestured helplessly at Erelah and her massive belly. "You."

Erelah had no idea what she meant. "I'm serious."

Rosalyn seemed to make a grand attempt at sobering up. "Of course. Erelah, every woman feels like she's blown up like a balloon when she's pregnant."

"Are you sure?" Erelah was certain she was anomalous in this regard.

"Very sure."

"I do not remember you being this large when you were with child," Erelah said. "And I have two more weeks to go in this pregnancy. It is… concerning."

Rosalyn's expression softened. "Erelah, honey… it's fine."

Erelah found little comfort in that. After all, what would Rosalyn say if things were truly amiss? What was there to do about it at this point? Her shoulders sagged.

Rosalyn frowned. "Okay, look. I have something to

show you." She held up a finger. "Just give me a minute, okay?"

Erelah nodded, and Rosalyn slipped off screen. While Erelah waited, she contemplated how little she knew about any of this. Had she had some sense about her, she would have known much earlier that Leksander was in love with her. Then they could have had some kind of normal mating ritual... although she couldn't imagine what that might be. Regardless, it wouldn't have comprised him turning wyvern, attacking her, then her having to hunt him down with her blade and liberate a demon from his mind. She was certain that normal couples did not have to endure such things. Normal couples would have time to discuss the intricacies of dragonling pregnancies before such an event was upon them. Then again, none of the princesses of the House of Smoke were any luckier than she. Arabella's mate attempted death before allowing her True Love to bloom. And then she was captured by Zephan, a despicable fae prince of the Winter Court, before her mate won her release. Rosalyn was even less lucky, having to risk her life to free Leonidas of his curse. Then Zephan intervened again, poisoning her and her baby with demon essence, such that the two nearly perished.

An overly large belly would be the least of their concerns.

By the time Rosalyn returned, Erelah was ready with an apology for wasting her time. But Rosalyn had brought another woman with her, one Erelah vaguely recognized... but the bulging belly she sported was all too familiar.

"Erelah, honey—do you remember Rachel?" Rosalyn asked. "She's Arabella's friend. Mated to Cinaed. He's—"

"A brave and good-hearted dragon," Erelah jumped in. "Yes, I know of him."

Rachel waved, beaming and giving Erelah's belly as wide-eyed a look as Erelah imagined was on her face. Then Rachel ran a hand over her belly as Erelah often did. "Guess we're going to have lots of dragon babies soon in the House of Smoke!"

"How long are you with child?" Erelah asked, glancing between their two forms.

"Four weeks. Same as you." She smiled. It was difficult to tell over the screen, plus the diminutive woman was shorter than Erelah, but their bellies seemed about the same size. Her breasts were swollen even larger than Erelah's, although she wasn't sure how large they were to begin with. It wasn't as if she needed to attend to these things.

But she nodded slowly. *This* was reassuring. "Does your baby move?" She wasn't sure if this was a proper question to ask.

"Hell yes," Rachel said. "Some days it feels like an entire rugby team in there!"

"Rugby?" Erelah asked Rosalyn.

"It's a sport." Rosalyn waved that off. "Doesn't matter. But you can see that you're both the same, right? Those strapping dragon men just make really robust babies. And you both are crazy gorgeous. Makes me wish I could do another dragonling."

"Anytime you're ready!" Leonidas's voice came from off-screen.

Rosalyn scowled in his direction. "We don't even know if that will work."

Leonidas edged into the corner of the screen. He looked weary but happy. "Yet, I am totally down for trying." He held baby Thorn in his arms, cradling the child, who was as beautiful as any angeling and radiated innocence in his sleep.

It was *that* sight which finally soothed her. Somehow the world ceased to matter—the danger, the treaty, the many forces who wished to stop her baby from breathing his first breath. All she wanted was to hold her own dragonling in her arms.

"Erelah, honey… are you okay?" Rosalyn's concern reached through the screen and drew her away from gazing at little Thorn.

"Yes." She was surprised to find tears glassing her view. She blinked them away. "Thank you," she said to Rosalyn. Then to Rachel, "The House of Smoke will be blessed with both our dragonlings."

"Well…" Rachel smirked. "Yours more than mine, Miss Angel. But okay."

"*No.*" Erelah said it a little too forcefully, judging by the shock on their faces. "My child will bring peace. A renewal of the treaty. But the whole reason for it—the whole reason for peace—is so dragonlings such as yours can be born."

"Okay, now… stop with that!" Rachel complained. "You're going to make me cry." She blinked and looked off-screen and wiped at her eyes. "Damn pregnancy hormones." She grumbled something else then trundled away. Leonidas went after her with the baby.

Only Rosalyn remained, but she was beaming. "I made *two* pregnant ladies cry today. Go me!"

"I did not cry." But Erelah could hardly contain her smile.

"Yes, you did. I saw you. Besides, aren't angelings always supposed to tell the truth?" she teased.

"That is the fae." Erelah tamed her smile. "Although, I do strive for the Truth in all things, occasionally a small lie is more important." She knew that a simple Truth existed even in falsehoods.

Rosalyn's smile slowly dimmed. Then she bit her lip

and nodded. "I wish I could be there to hold your hand when this baby comes, Erelah."

"I will be fine," she said with a smile.

"I know." Rosalyn nodded once to affirm this. "But you were there for me. You saved me… and my baby. I just wish… I wish there was something I could do."

"You have." Her smile grew. "And very soon our dragonlings will meet. And I will have need of your help then, princess of the House of Smoke."

"Yeah?" She brightened. "How so?"

"I was taken from my mother at birth. Raise in a cohort by an angel."

Rosalyn's expression took on a kind of horror.

Erelah smiled. "It was not so awful. But I never knew…" She struggled for the right words to explain. "This love that I have with Leksander. And now the baby. It is all new to me. I don't know how to… I don't know the proper way to raise a child."

"Sister, none of us do." Rosalyn reached to the screen and held her hand to it.

Erelah felt compelled to do the same.

"We'll figure it out together, okay?" Rosalyn said.

Erelah smiled. "Agreed."

Then they said their goodbyes, but for the first time since Erelah realized she was carrying this special soul in her womb, she finally felt… *at peace.*

She shuffled back to the bed, crawled across the expanse of it, then sunk down on her side, nestling up to one of the pillows. She had awoken not long ago, but already sleep was stealing over her again.

Two weeks.

In two weeks, she would carry her baby in her arms.

Chapter Twelve

ATER SLOSHED UP ON LEKSANDER'S CHEST.

He was sitting in a pool he had conjured in his great room, next to the windows where the sunlight streamed in and illuminated Erelah like a goddess. A true angel of light with pink-flushed skin and snow-white wings. A goddess who was riding his cock like she planned to ruin him with it.

And he was—utterly ruined for any other woman in the universe.

"Are you sure you're all right, my love?" he gasped out between her magic-assisted downward slams. It was possible he could drown under the waves she was making. They were certainly slopping over the sides, flooding the great room floor, and splashing the windows. But he was getting close… *so close*… he might also die if she stopped.

"Have I fatigued you, dragon prince?" she asked breathily as she slammed down on him. Her belly at the five-week mark was a hindrance to many of their favored positions. But as she gripped the edge of the pool, gaze tipped up to the window, lips parted, he suspected this might be a new favorite of hers. *He* definitely liked it when she took charge like this, pushing him down on the submerged bench and having her way with him.

"I can never get enough of you, angel girl." *God,* his voice was tight. Just like his balls. And his body. And the climax rushing at him. He slipped a hand to her nipple, already tight with the pleasure of riding him, and pinched. He slid the other hand down the tight round of her belly to where their bodies met—where she slid up and down his shaft. He found her nub and flicked, trying desperately to get her there before he—

She shifted her grip to rake her nails across his chest.

"Aahh!" he ground out. His climax rushed at him, taking him by surprise. He convulsed under her, gripping her hips under the water as she kept riding him. She was humming, then crying out softly, then louder... and louder...

He felt her climax work his cock as her angelsong shook the windows.

The sound faded.

Her movement slowed.

The water stopped threatening to drown him.

He slid his hands along her wet skin, marveling that she was here, carrying his child, still wrenching mind-blowing orgasms out of him. *Five weeks.* Nearly time for the baby... the tension of it was almost unbearable, so Leksander refused to think of it. They made love, ate, and slept. Even his check-ins with his brothers had dropped down to every three days. He lived in the moment—*loved* in the moment—and that was all that mattered.

Erelah settled in his lap, his cock still deep inside her. "The water is very pleasant," she murmured as she ran her fingers through his drenched hair.

"The water, hm?" He slid his hands up to cup her

breasts. "Not your mate? The one you just pounded into oblivion?"

She peered down at him over the swelling mounds of her breasts. She was well endowed *before* the pregnancy—now, it was like she was bursting with womanliness. Just the sight of her had him hard most of the time.

"My mate is also very pleasant." She grinned.

"Hm." He smirked and lifted her off his cock, separating their bodies. He'd conjured the water to be the perfect temperature on their skin, but it was nothing like the tight heat and magic when he was buried *inside* her. However, the water made it easier for him to float her slightly away, so he could slip off the pool bench and around behind her. "I think I want to strive for something more toe-curling than *pleasant.*" He reached from behind and guided her hands to grip the edge of the pool again. She was still facing the windows, but now she was standing with him behind her. His cock wasn't quite ready to follow up on this position, but soon. In the meantime, he slipped a hand between her legs.

She squirmed, rubbing her adorable bottom against his cock, but she didn't complain.

Neither did he.

The view out the window was mostly blue sky—from this angle, it was hard to see the sprawling forest below the keep. The tips of the nearest mountain tops were just visible. It was bright and hazy, and with absolutely no clouds in the sky, it was hard to picture there was anything but peace in the world.

Erelah was literally purring under his tender ministrations.

Or humming. Something. "What is that?" he asked.

"Angelsong," she whispered. She was still rubbing her

bottom against his front, and they had a nice little rhythm going now.

"Does it mean something?" He kept up with her but didn't rush it. He needed a little more time yet.

"Joy. Love. Peace." She stopped her seductive gyrations against him and twisted to look at him over her shoulder. "The baby sings too."

"Yeah?" The baby. *Their* baby. How quickly he had become used to the idea, yet still it was foreign and new. "I guess that makes sense. He'll be an angeling after all." Which also seemed strange. He'd relentlessly thought of the baby as a *dragonling.*

"And dragonling. He will be both." She gave him a single nod as if this was right and natural and good. It made sense—his father was a dragon and his mother an angeling.

At the same time, it was wondrous.

She smiled and turned to face the window, rubbing her delightful bottom against his now-stiffening cock. *Show time.*

He reached down to her hips—

Erelah's sharp intake of breath startled him. Then something *smacked* against the window just above him. His heart nearly jolted out of his body. Erelah reeled back into his arms, water splashing everywhere, and his brain could barely make sense of what he saw.

An angeling. Outside the window. He was falling away, tumbling head over heels, his blond hair and white wings catching the sun before he dropped out of sight.

Before Leksander could even react, a shadow angeling rocketed past the window, heading straight down, toward the falling angeling of light.

Erelah gasped. "Leksander!" She turned to him, eyes wide, the back of her hand pressed to her mouth.

Holy fuck, what was happening? He scrambled to pull her back from the window, but the water was slowing them down, dragging at them. He magicked the entire thing away then caught Erelah as she stumbled and nearly fell without the support of the water. He gathered her into his arms and retreated from the windows as far as they could… which was only to the entranceway.

She was shaking. He didn't know if it was cold or fear or anger—a wide-eyed fury was on her face—but he quickly magicked away the water from both their bodies and covered them with clothes.

"The shadow angelings are *here!*" Her eyes were dilated, and he was sure that was fear.

"They can't get in." He was sure that was true for angelings. But if they'd brought Elyon…

Erelah took a halting step toward the window.

"Erelah, no!" He tugged her back.

"That angeling…" She turned back, cheeks even more pale. "It was Tajael."

"What?" Now his eyes were wide. He looked back to the window. There was no more activity outside—none they could see, at least. But there could be a full on angeling war going on above the keep, and they might not see it.

As long as a stray body didn't slam into the window. An immortal body. Because it was the wards, not the window, that kept that angeling from sailing into their living room.

Anything else…

His stomach hollowed out. "Erelah." He grabbed hold of her shoulders to tear her worried gaze from the window. "It wasn't Tajael." Unless they'd brought the angeling back only to toss him off the roof—the last he'd heard, Tajael had been captured by the shadow angelings. But it made no sense to bring him here.

"He was—" She looked back to the window. "He seemed—"

"*Erelah.*"

Her attention whipped back to him.

"We have to get away from the windows."

Her eyes went wide, and she nodded rapidly. He took her by the hand and tried to think fast. Which room in his lair was furthest from the windows? From the roof? *Shit.* Virtually every room had a kind of window or skylight or some damn thing. He towed her away from the front door, down the side of the great room, and toward the guest room in the back. He never used it—it was tiny, meant for one—but it had no windows and was on the bottom floor, furthest from the roof. When he had the door closed behind him, he ran a hand through his hair.

"Shit." He looked back to the door. "I left the phone in the kitchen." He hesitated then waved her over to the bed in the corner. "You wait here. I'm going to run out, get the phone, and I'll be right back."

She pursed her lips together but turned and strode quickly over to the bed. Before she was even sitting, he was tearing out of the room, dashing across his lair, and going for the phone. Internally, he was cursing the whole way. Erelah didn't know Tajael had been captured. She didn't know about the ongoing demon uprising in Seattle. Or that an angeling war was raging in the world outside the keep. His brothers were supposed to be *handling* this. And if they weren't—if there were fucking *angelings* smashing into his window—then things had to have gotten worse outside.

Much worse.

He grabbed the phone and dialed on his way back to the guest room. A quick glance at the window showed no more angelings. But that meant nothing.

Erelah sat cross-legged on the bed, cradling her belly as

if she could protect the baby with her arms. Leksander's heart cringed at the sight, but he closed the door behind him and paced the room while he waited for Lucian to pick up.

He wasn't picking up.

"Fuck!" He tapped that off and dialed Leonidas. Still nothing.

"It was Tajael," Erelah said quietly. "I'm sure of it."

"It wasn't Tajael." He flipped through his contacts. Who could he call?

Erelah was nodding to herself. "He would defend us. He would be the last on the line. They would have to fight through him—"

"It *wasn't* Tajael." Leksander found Rosalyn's number and dialed.

Erelah frowned at him and slowly rose from the bed. "How do you know?"

He was saved from answering by Rosalyn picking up on the first ring. "Leksander?" Her voice was strung tight.

"What the hell is happening?" he demanded. "There's an angeling fight outside our window!"

"Oh, shit." She let out a breath that sounded like she was on the move. "Leonidas is supposed to be back from the patrols. I told him not to go. I *told* him!" He heard a baby crying in the background. Then the sound rushed closer. "It's okay, sweetie. It's all right."

Leksander rubbed his face with the hand not holding the phone. "Okay, you... you just take care of Thorn. We're sitting tight here. Call me when you know something."

"Okay." The phone was muffled. The baby's crying had quieted, but the small sounds of upset were a lot closer. Rosalyn must have picked him up. "They can't get through the wards," she said, meaning the angelings. "And

I know Leonidas won't drop the wards to come inside. Not with angelings outside and our babies in here."

"No," Leksander agreed quickly. He shouldn't be panicking Rosalyn any more than necessary. "No, you're safe in your lair. Stay there. We'll do the same."

"I'll call you if I hear anything." The phone line clicked off.

Erelah was scanning his face, so he quickly relayed the phone conversation. "Whatever this is, they're fighting it," Leksander assured her. "They've got Markos and his angelings. They can hold them off." He swallowed and prayed that was true. Then he stuffed the phone in his pocket and gathered his mate into his arms. "They can't get through to us. I promise."

"The wards are holding." Her voice was surprisingly calm.

"Yeah. You saw it." If nothing else, an angeling of light crashed into their windows and *bounced off*. If it was just the windows, they would have shattered with that kind of impact. But that didn't mean the shadow forces wouldn't get creative and try something. Leksander pulled back to look at Erelah's troubled face. "The wards are holding, and I don't think that shadow angeling saw us. But they might try crashing something through—"

"Like the tree at the cave." Her cheeks were so pale.

"Like the tree. Or… something else." He didn't even want to speak his fears at this point because they were too alive in his mind. "We'll just stay away from the windows until this is handled."

She pulled back from him. "That angeling…"

He winced.

"How do you *know* he's not Tajael?" She was giving him a steely-eyed look.

He wouldn't be able to squirm his way out of this. And

with angelings crashing into the window… she might as well know the truth. "I can't be sure," he admitted. "But supposedly, Tajael was captured by the shadow realm."

Her eyes widened in horror.

"There's a lot of fighting going on," he rushed out. "They may have just taken him prisoner. I mean, they're out there having a war. They probably don't have time to—"

"How long?" she cut him off.

He swallowed. "How long for—"

"Leksander." She was *pissed.* "How long have you been keeping this from me? How long has Tajael been captured?"

He straightened. Better to take his lumps straight out. "About two weeks. Things have been going badly on the outside. Demon uprising. Angeling war in Seattle." He couldn't help glancing at the door. "And apparently now here."

She shook her head, slowly, her hand reflexively covering her belly. She took a step back, and then another.

"Erelah, I would have told you, but—"

"No," she said, gaze distant as she backed up and slowly sat on the bed. "You were protecting me. And the baby." She wasn't looking at him.

He hurried to her side and dropped to his knees. Then he scooped up her hands and waited until she finally dragged her gaze to meet his. "I'm sorry, my love. But no matter what, *no one* is getting in this lair. I promise you that."

She nodded, but it was vacant. Tears shimmered in her eyes as she looked away. "Tajael is lost. Humanity is suffering. Angelings are…" She choked up and looked back, her beautiful face twisted up with the effort of holding back those tears. "It is as foretold. The End Times."

"*No.*" But a rush of fear went through him. Could she be right? Was merely daring to try to have this angeling child already tearing things apart? "I can't believe that. Not now."

She examined his face. Tears crested and raced each other down her face. She put a hand to his cheek. "We *must* survive, Leksander."

Relief gushed through him. "I know."

"Everything depends on our baby." She rested a hand on her belly between them. "We shall avenge Tajael by *surviving.*" The grief on her face was killing him.

"He might still be—"

"He is lost." She dropped her gaze and shook her head. "He wouldn't allow them to get this close if he still lived."

Leksander wanted to argue that maybe Tajael was still captured. Maybe he simply *couldn't.* But then that would mean Tajael had been in the shadow realm for *weeks*... and Leksander couldn't imagine any angeling of light surviving that long. Not even Tajael.

His phone rang from his pocket, startling them both. He hurried to fish it out. "Yeah?" he said quickly, not even checking the caller.

It was Rosalyn. "They're okay. Your brothers. They're back inside the keep."

"So the fight's over then?"

"Yes," Rosalyn said. "For now."

Leksander didn't know exactly what that meant, but he gave Erelah a reassuring nod.

She lay down on the bed, curling over on her side. His heart ached more with each tear that slid down her face. He stood and stepped back.

"What happened?" Leksander demanded more quietly as he stepped to the far side of the room.

"I guess the shadow angelings somehow cloaked and took everyone by surprise when Leonidas and Lucian returned to the keep. Your brothers managed to keep them out, but the angelings of light were trapped inside. Others had to be called in from the patrols to help."

"But Lucian and Leonidas are all right?" he asked.

"Yeah." He could hear the relief in her voice. "And those shadow bastards took off as soon as Leonidas dropped the wards and allowed Markos to get *out* of the keep to join the fight."

"So everything's clear?"

"I think so."

Leksander swallowed. "All right. Here's the thing. I'm not bringing Erelah and the baby near any windows or anywhere on the second level of my lair. That's right under the roof." And he remembered all too well when he had gone mad in his wyvern form—he'd literally torn a hole through it. Magic had fixed the roof, but it was just too close.

"Good idea."

"Tell Leonidas we need some kind of reinforcement— physical reinforcement—around my lair. I don't want anything getting in that just happens not to be made of magic." He didn't really want to say *what* out loud with Erelah listening. Guns. Poison. Rocket launchers, for fuck's sake. They could put anything through the windows—hell, even the walls—if they were determined enough.

And he was sure they were determined enough.

Erelah didn't move from her quiet crying on the bed.

"You got it," Rosalyn said. "As soon as everything's settled down, they'll get right on it."

"Thanks. Keep me in the loop." Then he swiped the phone closed and hustled over to the bed. It was entirely too small for two people, much less one oversized dragon prince and a very pregnant angeling.

But Leksander slid in next to Erelah, anyway…

And just held her while she cried.

Chapter Thirteen

 Erelah asked. Was he serious?

"Dragonlings are notoriously on time," Leksander replied. "Gestation is so fast that each day is almost like a week. So where humans might be a week early or late, that's only a day for dragons." He shuffled around the pastries and fruits on the tray in front of her—he'd left it sitting on the couch, perhaps in hopes she would eat more, but her body rebelled at the thought. At six weeks into this pregnancy—exactly, in an hour—her belly presented a challenge to seeing, moving, sitting, or just about any other activity. And food was utterly contemptible.

She was sure there was no room inside her except for this child.

And he only grew more active as each day wore on.

And they had been *long* days. The past week—since she'd learnt of Tajael's death, the angeling war raging outside, and the possible End of Times approaching— she'd slept more than any other in her life. Their love- making had ceased for the simple reason that she couldn't bear it—as if joy had died at that moment, along with her steadfast friend. Tajael was the only person other than Leksander whom she had thought of as her family. Even Markos, her faction leader and substitute father, didn't hold her heart the way Tajael had. And no other angeling had ever been a more fierce friend.

She hoisted her belly around so she could sit straighter on the couch. "So I should be giving birth within the hour."

Leksander scowled at the uneaten food but started gathering it up anyway. "Well, it's not that precise."

"And this is an angeling," she reminded him. "I'm unsure the gestation time on those." Somehow, it had never been important to learn. "Perhaps the birth will be delayed."

Leksander grimaced and carried the food away. She could hardly stand the thought herself. *More* time in this purgatory? It might drive her mad. She attempted to banish that thought from her mind. No good could come of such morose thinking. But her dark mood lingered. Somehow, it did not feel as if the baby were about to be born. She'd discussed it with Rachel and knew all the facts of dragon-human hybrids and their pregnancies. But she was *angeling*… and so was her child.

There was no knowing this before it happened.

Leksander returned from the kitchen and held his hands out to her. "Come walk for a bit."

She had no desire to move, but it was supposed to encourage the baby to come. So she took his help in gaining liberation from the couch.

He kept one hand in hers but slipped the other to the small of her back, as if he expected her to topple over. She was ungainly, but not that much. Yet she allowed it.

Perhaps the fever of their lovemaking was quenched by the sorrow in her heart, but his touch still held magic—and not just the electric, erotic kind. It was a soothing feeling. A security that said, *You're safe*, as much or more as the welded metal that covered the windows. It now felt as if they lived inside a box—but it was a secure box, hardened against anything the shadow angelings might decide to ram through the magical wards which protected her and the baby.

She took small steps… because there was nowhere to go but the same well-worn path she'd been traveling. Through the great room. Down the hall to the guest room. Back to the kitchen. Leksander didn't like it when she went up the stairs to the bedroom, so she stayed below and slept in the guest room. He curled next to her at first then took to sleeping on the floor next to the bed.

Between her and the door.

He'd brought the large screen down from the bedroom and installed it in the living room so he could communicate with his brothers about the outside world.

None of it was good.

The baby gave a sizeable kick as she rounded the corner into the kitchen. She teetered slightly, and Leksander braced her. It was hardly awkward—they'd spent so much time doing this walking routine, they had a dance about it. Easy and comfortable. Another way he soothed her with his simple presence. It helped her to forget the world outside where mortal and immortal fires were threatening to burn it down.

They walked through the kitchen and exited out into the hall. "Do your brothers know the hour approaches?" she asked.

"Yeah. Rosalyn is on standby to guide you via the screen. If you want." He peered at her.

Of course, no one was going in or out of the lair to come help her. Leksander alone would help her deliver the child. Strangely, that part didn't frighten her as it probably should. She'd attended the births of Thorn and Larik. She knew what to expect in terms of pain and difficulty for herself. That was of no concern. Her only concern was that something might go wrong with the child.

"It would be good to have her guidance," Erelah said. She had discussed this out of Leksander's hearing. If there were problems with the birth, Rosalyn was to instruct Leksander to take the baby with her blade. Or his talons. Long ago, Lucian had used his dragon talons to slice open his mate's belly when the baby was in distress. The baby and mate had both perished, but it needn't be so for her baby. Erelah might not survive the surgery, but the child was fully formed. He could exist on his own. If her body didn't see fit to release him, Rosalyn had vowed to make Leksander go through with it.

Hopefully, it would not come to that.

They crossed the hall and circled the great room, passing the walled-up windows on the way. "Has there been an attack yet today?" she asked as they headed toward the back bedroom. It was already past noon, and every day of the last week had seen another bout of shadow angelings testing the barriers of the keep, both magical and physical.

"No." Leksander grimaced, and she knew he didn't wish to discuss it. But the hour approached for her baby to come. She felt certain the attacks must escalate.

"Has Markos recalled his angelings from Seattle?" Part of the plan was to reinforce the keep in the final hours. She'd had to force that information from Leksander, but it was a solid plan.

"Yes." They reached the guest room, which was small,

but they made the circuit in there regardless, using up every square inch of travel in the lair.

"How many did we lose in yesterday's attack?" She knew angelings were falling each day in defense of her and her baby. Some were Falling to shadow, mostly due to Wrath but also when sickened by shadow blade strikes. Some simply were killed. Elyon had yet to show his face, coward that he was, leaving his dark angelings to relentlessly siege the keep. No matter how many were cut down, he seemed to have an endless supply. Markos, on the other hand, had far fewer—and dwindling—numbers. This war had cost many lives already.

Leksander was taking his time in answering, guiding her back out through the guest bedroom door. Only at her insistent look did he answer. "Seven." Then he hastily added, "But the troops recalled from the city are in the dozens, plus Markos has gotten more help from two other angels of light. They've sent more angelings."

Erelah nodded. The angels rarely interacted—they kept to their separate Dominions—but angelings would often move from one Dominion to another. It was not as if angels of the light were enemies of anything other than shadow. And angels would "lend" their angeling troops to one another. But for them to ally together in fighting this menace would be much more significant. *A sign of war.* The Warrior Angels themselves could come out of their retirement, but that fury would only be unleashed if a heavenly war were actually upon them. Such a move would pull more than just Elyon into this... the other angels of darkness might also rise up.

Erelah could see why Markos would hesitate to ask for such help.

With any luck, it would prove unnecessary. They had gotten this far. With horrible casualties among angelings

—including Tajael—but overall, the losses were still small.

Small, yet the cost was already too high.

They had reached the living room once more. She squeezed Leksander's hand and released him, moving back toward the couch. The fatigue washed through her, inspired by thoughts she should, by all rights, banish. She could properly mourn Tajael once the baby was born.

The baby kicked even as she settled into the couch. She patted her rounded belly. "Soon, little one. Soon, you will be free."

The love in Leksander's eyes as he sat with her banished some of the darkness in her heart.

"Does he want out?" he asked with a smile in his eyes.

"With the amount of kicking? I would say yes." She rested her hands lightly on her belly.

Leksander bent down to kiss the backs of them. Then, as if speaking to their son, he said, "We're all waiting on you, buddy. Any time you're ready."

The baby rustled around in response then hummed a little baby angelsong.

The darkness lifted from her heart. She was sure it would return, but for the moment, she was filled only with joy. She reached for Leksander, encouraging him to lay his head on her belly to hear the babysong. When he did, a smile spread on his face that brought her even more happiness.

Then a buzzing sounded that Erelah quickly recognized as Leksander's phone.

He sat up and pulled it out of his pocket. "Yeah?" He quickly frowned and flicked his hand toward the screen. It had been mounted where the windows had been covered with steel reinforcements. Leonidas's frowning face appeared, and Leksander quickly rose up to go speak to him. It took a moment longer for Erelah to struggle up from the couch on her own.

"We've got a situation here," Leonidas started. He hesitated when Erelah came to Leksander's side, now visible on screen.

"What is it?" she asked.

Leksander slipped his arm around her shoulders. "Spit it out, Leonidas. I can't keep anything from her anymore."

Leonidas sighed. "All right. But you're not going to like it." He paused as if choosing his words. "Zephan's outside the keep."

Leksander scowled. "But the wards are holding, right?"

"Yeah." But Leonidas still looked pensive. "We've got the main ones around the keep. Then a separate sectional ward that encases the royal lairs, covering all three baby dragon princes. And of course, you've got your fucking death wards around your lair in particular. That's three sets. He's outside all of them."

"Is he trying to magic his way inside?" Erelah asked. Fae were not as powerful as angels; more like angelings in raw magical strength. Even a single set of wards should keep him out.

"No," Leonidas said, then bit his lip.

"Leonidas." There was a warning in Leksander's voice.

His brother just shook his head and looked to Erelah. "He's got Tajael."

"What?" Her eyes went wide. "But I thought—"

"Nope. He's beaten all to hell but definitely *not* dead." Leonidas grimaced. "So there's that."

Leksander was leaning away from the screen, a horror-filled look on his face. "He wants to trade." It was a whisper.

"Trade?" Erelah asked quickly, looking from Leonidas to Leksander. What did he mean? "Trade for what?"

Leksander growled. "He has to be crazy if he thinks—"

"He's not asking to trade Tajael for Erelah. I mean, Zephan's an asshole, but he's not an idiot." Leonidas had his hands up, reassuring. "I don't know exactly what he wants, but he's offering up Tajael like some kind of lure. And he wants to talk to you—to Leksander—so maybe then he'll say what he really wants. But he has to know there's no way we're just going to give him Erelah. Or the baby. Or really anything else."

Leksander's eyes narrowed. "He just wants to *talk?*"

"Well, he's jittery as fuck," Leonidas said. "Which is really a disturbing look on a fae prince. I'm sure he wants *something,* but he won't say unless it's face-to-face with you." Leonidas shot Erelah a look. "I'm sorry, Erelah, but we can't just give him whatever. Not if it endangers you or the babies."

"No, of course not." But her heart was aching all anew. *Tajael was alive!* But what had the fae done to him? And how could he be in fae hands at all? "But Zephan wouldn't give a care for Larik or Thorn. Their births already set the magic in motion for the treaty to renew. He gains nothing by slaying them. Or you and Lucian. Or your mates. There is only one thing he could be after... and it is *my* child."

"*Exactly.*" Leonidas looked relieved. "Leksander, whatever it is, it's a trap."

"I know." But Leksander's eyes were narrowed, calculating. "We just have to make it a trap for *Zephan.*"

Leonidas looked at his brother like he was crazed.

Erelah likewise leaned away. "This is not the time for revenge."

"Not revenge," Leksander said, and the cool calculation was still on his face. "A *solution...* to all this." He turned to face Leonidas. "Think about it. The demon uprising in Seattle. The shadow angelings fighting to prevent the angelings of light from fixing it. This all sources back to Zephan. He's involved in all of it. If we could take him out…"

"Take him *out?*" Leonidas's expression went from *You're crazy* to *You're not even making sense now.* "He's a prince of the Winter Court. What are you going to do, bite him?"

"No." The coolness on Leksander's face didn't waver. "I'm going to kill him with an angel blade."

Erelah's mouth dropped open. "That is too much danger! You can't just—"

"Erelah." He turned to her and held her by the shoulders. "You need to have this baby. But you don't actually need *me.* You're strong. You can do this. As long as you and the baby are out of Zephan's reach, you'll be fine. The death wards will protect you, but once they're broached… I'm dead. And I don't want to be dead. I want to live to see our son grow up and struggle to find a mate of his own."

She couldn't believe he was saying these words. "There's no sense in this risk!"

Even Leonidas looked aghast.

"Yes, there is." And she could see the fire lighting up Leksander's eyes now. "If we can lure Zephan in and destroy him, all of this goes away. All the threats. All the risk. Don't you see? All along, it's always been Zephan. He attacked my brothers. He attacked *me…* infected me with demon and turned me to wyvern. But he can't *kill* me, my love. I'm protected by the treaty. But *I* can kill *him.* Given a blade infused with angel power. And once I do… this End of Times you so fear will stop. All of it. Because it's been Zephan's doing all along."

She was shaking her head, but she could see it was no use. He had already decided. And, in a way, it made sense.

Zephan *had* been there at every turn. He *was* responsible for the demon uprising throwing the world into chaos and pitting light against shadow. Maybe her child would show that angelings of light could mate and still stay in the light. But the angels and angelings still must *choose* that path… and maybe they wouldn't if the world wasn't in such chaos with angelings dying by the handfuls. If Zephan wasn't recruiting the shadow realm to relentlessly come after her and her child.

Once the baby was born, maybe this would all end. Or maybe Zephan would have already tipped the immortal world into a war they couldn't pull back from. But if Zephan was destroyed… the baby could come, and all would return to peace.

Leksander was waiting for her blessing. And if it were *her*, with a chance to save the worlds and the man she loved, she would easily do it. She couldn't say no to him wanting to do the same.

"All right." It took all her energy to say those two words.

Leksander gave her a sharp nod.

"You're both fucking crazy," Leonidas said, but not in a way that disapproved.

"I'm putting up another set of wards," Leksander said to his brother, but with a side look at her. "Just around Erelah and the baby, in the guest room, within the lair. That's *four* levels of wards, two of which are death wards. No one is getting through that."

Leonidas just shook his head.

Erelah sought Leksander's hand. "I must keep my blade, but you can get another from Markos. Bring Tajael to your side. Give him the blade and let him strike first. Take no unnecessary chances."

"I promise."

And she believed him. She knew his love would bring him back.

He arranged with Leonidas to meet him at the throne room, the least protected part of the keep. And suddenly, it felt certain that the baby would come while Leksander was gone. As if she was sure the fates would conspire to put her into labor the exact moment he stepped out of the lair.

"The screen," she said, gesturing to it as she went to retrieve her blade from the desk. "I might need it."

"I'll move it to the bedroom." He quickly worked to magic it and its connections away from the wall, trans- porting it to the guest bedroom. He set it up there. The room was as warm as it normally was, but a shiver had taken up residence deep in her bones.

Why had she agreed to this?

Once he was done with the screen, she slipped into his arms and grabbed hold of him with one hand, her angel blade gripped in the other. "This is madness. Don't go. Wait for the baby to come."

He hugged her back then slowly extricated himself from her grasp. "I know Zephan. He has something planned with this. Some last trick up his sleeve." He held her cheeks in his hands. "Trust me, I know this. But he won't stop until *someone stops him.* Do you understand what I'm saying? He's relentless. And now that we're down to the last hours with this baby, he may become… *desperate.*"

"Desperate?" What did he think Zephan might do?

"Desperate enough that anything is in play. As long as I can control some of this, I've got the upper hand. I have a chance at stopping him and whatever he has planned. Just trust me, okay?" He quickly kissed her forehead. "I'm coming back to raise that baby to be a kickass dragon. Can't have too much angeling influence over him."

She smiled through the pain in her heart, but it was still difficult to let him go.

He kissed her once more then left through the bedroom door. After it clicked shut, she could hear him conjuring wards just outside. Then his shoes scuffed the floor and retreated.

She was alone—just her, her baby, and her blade.

Chapter Fourteen

The throne room was crowded.

Leksander counted at least twenty-five angelings, most female, but that hardly mattered—their strength came in their angel powers. As Erelah had shown him often, female angelings kicked ass just as hard the male ones. His brothers, Lucian and Leonidas, stood nervously watching them and their drawn angel blades, but it was Markos whose power dominated the room.

And he was key in all this. Not least in making sure Leksander didn't die. His death wards would go with him, leaving Erelah with only two layers of standard wards between her and the world outside. Standard wards were enough to keep out fae like Zephan, but who knew what Elyon and his dark forces had cooked up while regularly assaulting them. Leksander meant to keep his promise to his mate—staying alive while stopping Zephan was critical.

The oversized angel waited for him to approach, standing near the throne dais at the far end. Leksander dodged the flexed wings and tightly gripped blades and strode up to the front.

As he drew near, Markos produced an angel blade from somewhere in the skimpy toga the angels always wore. "You will need this." He handed it over, and the power of it thrummed in Leksander's hand. "I've given it my strongest blessing. A warrior's power is contained in that blade."

Leksander wasn't sure what that meant, but he would take whatever advantage he could. "Thank you." He conjured a sheath strapped to his leg and holstered it there. He knew how to wield a blade, but this one was more dangerous than talons... or any other weapon he'd used. He turned to his brothers. "What's the status with Zephan?"

"He's hanging out at the weigh station with Tajael," Leonidas said.

"And he still wants inside the keep?" Leksander asked. "Face-to-face with me, before he says what this is all about?"

Lucian nodded. "The fae can't lie, but this fucker hasn't told the truth a day in his life. What's your plan with this?"

"We get him in here," Leksander said, "then I kill him."

Leonidas cocked an eyebrow. "Gee, I wish I'd thought of that before."

"I'm not saying it will be *easy*," Leksander snarled. He turned to Markos. "I could use some help on this."

"I cannot kill a fae without cause." Markos's face was impassive.

"Cannot or will not?" Leksander grumbled. "And besides, we have plenty of cause. For starters, he infected me with demon—"

"That is insufficient," Markos coolly interrupted him. "The fae are the avowed enemies of the light. They traffic in demons. They have no reverence for life—human or angel. But if I were to strike him down without direct cause—either in defense of a human life or self-defense—then I would succumb to Wrath almost immediately. I am useless to you in shadow, prince of the House of Smoke. Not to mention that I am unwilling to commit such a Vice."

"Oh, for fuck's sake!" Leonidas said. "What about all the angelings we've lost? Doesn't that count?"

"Zephan is not responsible for that," Markos said. "That we know of."

"The hell he isn't!" Leksander said. "How can you—"

Markos held up his hand, but it was the not-so-subtle pulse of power from him that cut Leksander off. "If I have direct knowledge that Zephan has declared war on my angelings, or should he strike one down before me, then I will be free to act as Warrior Angel in defense of humanity or angelkind. But not before."

Leksander scrubbed his face, trying to wipe away the frustration. "Do we have to let Zephan kill someone before you're willing to act?"

"Before I'm *able* to act," Markos said. "Without turning shadow. As I said—"

"Yeah, yeah," Leonidas said, disgust written on his face. "You're useless to us then. Seems like you're pretty useless to us *now.*"

Markos didn't answer, just gave his brother a cool look, but Leksander's mind was spinning. Arguing against Virtues was no way to get anywhere with an angel. That much he knew.

And he definitely needed Markos's protection. "Maybe you *can* help," he said. All attention turned to him. He pulled his angel blade and pointed it at Markos. The angel looked mildly amused. "You can't *kill*

Zephan… but you can bless the blade *I'll* use to kill him."

"You will need it for self-defense, especially against a foe as strong as the fae." But his expression soured into annoyance.

"Right. Defense." Leksander had watched Erelah struggle with her light and shadow natures, and he suspected he understood the distinction better than Markos, an angel of the light who had never been shadow—never had to truly struggle. Erelah *decided* to return from the shadow. He watched love banish the darkness—and not just any love, but the *love of oneself.* Something these angels and their kind had serious issues with. But believing they were righteous—having faith they were serving a pure and just cause—*that* was what kept them in the light. So, no matter what, Leksander had to make sure Markos still *believed* he was acting according to the Virtues or his principles or whatever. Because it would, in fact, be a fucking disaster if he turned shadow in the middle of things.

"Okay." Leksander sheathed the blade. "So you can give me a blade, but you personally can't kill Zephan unless he directly threatens to kill me or my brothers or one of the angelings. Then, and only then, you can strike him down. Right?"

"That is correct." Markos's cool demeanor had returned. Good.

"Zephan can't kill me outright—not as long as the treaty holds—but he has *something* planned." Leksander knew that was the truth. "And while he can't kill me, he can kill the *hell* out of your angelings. Including Erelah, who *has* to be his target."

Markos frowned and nodded.

"Protecting Erelah is paramount." Leksander gestured vaguely around the throne room to the invisible wards still protecting them—normal wards tied to his brothers, or really anyone with sworn allegiance to the House of Smoke. Any of the three of them in the throne room could pull them down. "Once we bring down the wards, once Zephan is inside, that's when he has a chance to do something. To make his move. He may fight his way out of this throne room, trying to go after Erelah. He may do something completely different. Whatever it is, it's *not* in our interest to let that happen. Maybe you can't kill him without provocation… but you can definitely *bind him* so he can't carry through on whatever mischief he has planned."

Markos's eyebrows lifted. "I could bind him in a way that would prevent him from using his magic. He would be unharmed but restrained."

"Yes!" Leksander said. "That is what I'm talking about." With Zephan restrained, Leksander would have no qualms about plunging an angel blade into the asshole's heart. Markos could stand back and watch, but he had better not get in the way.

It didn't sound like he would, though. And if he did… Leksander would fight that battle when it came.

"I like this idea." Leonidas caught his gaze, and an understanding passed between them. His brother knew *exactly* what Leksander had planned. A small nod from Lucian said he got the message, too.

Good. Everyone was on board with this. *And fuck Zephan.* He should never have messed with the House of Smoke and their mates in the first place. "All right, then. Here's how this will work. We can pull down the wards around the keep to let Zephan in. I'm not worried about him breaking the other three levels of wards—we already know fae magic isn't strong enough for that." Lucian gave him a nod—they had proved that specifically for Zephan when the two of them trapped the fae in Lucian's tomb, with all three inside. Zephan had no choice but to vow not to kidnap or otherwise harm Lucian's mate—and a fae's promise is magically binding. "So, Zephan we can manage, but when we bring down the outer wards to let him in, we give a small moment of time for the shadowkind to get in too." He turned to face Markos. "I want you at my side, protecting me during that moment. My death means the death wards protecting Erelah come down. I can't have that happen."

Markos tipped his head in agreement.

Leksander turned to his brothers. "Okay, I'm going to conjure a personal shield around Markos and me." Not as strong as a ward but enough to give them momentary protection if Elyon suddenly materialized in the throne room. "You bring down the outer wards, get Zephan and Tajael in, then raise them again. I'll drop my shield as soon as that's done."

Lucian and Leonidas nodded their agreement.

Leksander stepped closer to Markos and raised a shimmering shield of magic around the two of them. "Okay, let's let the bastard in."

Leonidas briefly closed his eyes. Lucian tensed, and Leksander rested his hand on his blade, ready for literally anything. He couldn't reach with his fae senses past his fae-magic-generated shield, but Zephan—who was an *actual* fae—must have been probing the wards, watching and waiting for them to come down. A half-second later, the air popped and light flashed, announcing his arrival in the throne room.

A split moment after that, Leonidas gave him a nod. "Wards up."

Leksander exhaled a low breath and dropped the shield around Markos and him.

Tajael was by Zephan's side, held up only by his grip

on the angeling's arm. The fae shoved him away in disgust, and Tajael fell to his knees, head hanging down.

Sweet mother of magic, he looked bad. Dark, inky blade slices—deep ones—all over his front and back. His wings were half white, half shadow, and it looked like the darkness was winning some kind of creeping war of attrition. Leksander reached out with his fae senses—the angeling even *tasted* of the shadow side, but at least he was alive.

Lucian went to help Tajael up. "You all right?"

Tajael nodded but said nothing. Just that motion seemed like it took all his strength. Lucian half carried him back to his throne, settling Tajael into the seat. He looked ready to pass out.

"Nice of you to return our angeling," Leksander said bitterly. "After you beat the hell *into* him. Now, what exactly did you want to talk about?" He flicked a look to Markos. The angel was standing impassively by his side, doing nothing except stare in horror at Tajael. Specifically, he was *not* binding Zephan. What was he waiting for?

"Send out the angel," Zephan said stiffly. "And raise the wards again. Then we'll talk."

What? Leksander swung back to peer at the fae prince. What game was he playing? "You're not giving the orders around here, Zephan." Leksander's hand slid to grip the hilt of his blade. Should he just go for it? No. Zephan could easily blast him across the room. He had to be bound first. Leksander gave a pointed look to Markos, but he wasn't paying attention. His eyes were focused on Tajael. Leksander swung his gaze to the throne—Tajael was half passed out.

"Is he going to make it?" Leksander asked.

It was a general question, but Markos answered. "He's very close to turning shadow."

Oh, for the love of magic… Whether Tajael was in shadow

or not was the *least* of their problems. "Look," Leksander said to Markos, "we can heal Tajael later, all right?" He gestured to Zephan, but Markos still didn't respond, just narrowed his gaze further at Tajael.

"Well, I certainly hope he'll survive," sniffed Zephan. "I went to a lot of trouble to bring him here." The fae looked as awkward—and amazingly *not* arrogant—as Leksander had ever seen him.

"What the hell are you talking about, Zephan?" Leonidas asked. He was also giving *What the fuck? What are you waiting for?* side looks to Leksander.

"I knew you wouldn't let me in if I arrived empty-handed," Zephan said, the grumble and reluctance in his voice bringing Leksander's attention back to him. "Especially after I, well, was a little *overzealous* in my treatment of the princes of the House of Smoke."

"*Overzealous?*" Leksander spat. "Are you fucking kidding me?" What the hell was this? Zephan trying to con them with a last-minute, error-of-his-ways apology? No way. Leksander was killing this asshole *dead* for what he'd already done—just as soon as Markos got his shit together and actually bound the fae.

Zephan pulled a face like he'd swallowed the bullshit he was trying to feed to them. "I don't expect a mere dragon to understand, but I had my reasons, prince of the House of Smoke. I was taking the most expedient route to preventing the treaty from renewing. I didn't mean for..." He gestured in a flailing kind of way at Markos. "This whole thing to spiral out of control. I should have known better than to trust an *angel.*" He spat the word, and he threw a glare at Markos, but somehow, that wasn't directed at the angel of light. Markos had finally drawn his gaze away from Tajael to give an amused look to Zephan.

"What the hell are you saying?" Leksander asked. And

now he was seriously confused, because if Zephan wasn't the one inciting the angel war… then who was?

"Elyon." Zephan ground the name out. "He's coming, and he's not exactly pleased, so for the love of magic, will you please send this angel out to give us a fighting chance?" He squinted at Markos. "If you're as clever as you think, dragon prince, you'd let the angels fight it out while we wait to see the victor." He turned back to Leksander. "I am hoping your angel of light will win… as long as it's far away from any space, mortal or immortal, that I happen to be occupying."

Leksander leaned back and peered at Zephan. "You're just trying to save your own skin."

"Well, of course." Zephan looked at him like was crazy. "Did you expect something different?"

A strangled laugh erupted from Leksander. "No."

"Then get on with it, if you would." Zephan glared at him.

"Hang on." Leonidas stepped away from the throne dais and down to the main floor with Leksander, Zephan, Markos… and a host of edgy angelings. There were a couple dozen angel blades pointed in the fae's direction. "If you've managed to piss off Elyon, and he's coming here to get you, why shouldn't we just toss you outside, raise the wards, and let him finish you off?"

Zephan bared his teeth. "Because I'm *helping you,* you idiot. Do you think your wards will hold him off for long? I'm telling you, his angelings have been probing for weaknesses in your magic for a week. He'll find a way inside. And then the battle will be fought within your walls, where your precious mates and beast children reside. Send the light angel out to stop him. In return, I can tame the demon outbreak in Seattle. I know you dragons worry about your precious human breeding stock. But Elyon is a bigger threat than you realize. He has angels of darkness ready to unleash. I thought I could…" He visibly swallowed, and Leksander had never seen this wild-eyed look on his face. "I thought I could *contain* him. I thought we could do business together. But this shadow realm… *reason* is not Elyon's forte, and simply suspending the treaty is nowhere near enough to satisfy him."

"So you've unleashed a monster on us all," Leksander said, the full horror of this sinking in. "Good fucking job, Zephan."

The fae prince cringed. He swung a look to Lucian, then Leonidas, then back to Leksander. "I know I've wronged each of you in turn. I don't expect you to understand my noble pursuit of a better world without a treaty hampering the business of fae and dragon alike—" He held up a hand at the *What the fuck?* expression on Leksander's face. "Regardless of that… when I turned you wyvern, Leksander Smoke, I truly believed I would finally prevail. But you dragons are obnoxiously stubborn in your mate selection and your *love.*" He drawled the word out like it was poison. "An angeling who can turn a wyvern back to dragon? Clearly, the fates were conspiring against me. I'm done fighting you this round—I'll just wait you out, House of Smoke. The fae live a very long time, far longer than these beast spawn you've created. Their time will come, and so will mine. But there will be nothing for us to haggle about if we're all destroyed. Elyon has more in mind… dangerous things, dragon prince. Now, don't be a fool. Send these angelkind out to fight this battle and let them spend their energy on each other. Then you and I can live to spar another day."

Leksander really didn't want to believe a word of this. Zephan was giving up? He would try next time? The red haze of anger that welled up—the very idea that Zephan would go after the children, once they were grown—almost had him lunging forward and burying his blade in Zephan's chest.

The problem was… it made too much sense.

Zephan couldn't hope to win with Markos here—and he had to have known the angel was in the keep. And yet… Zephan came unarmed. With Tajael as a bargaining chip. And he just assumed they would protect him now that his alliance with an insane shadow angel had gone south.

Only Zephan could be that arrogant and not even blink.

Leksander looked to Markos. "What do you think?" He needed the angel on board no matter what.

"I think this fae lies in spite of his species being bound to Truth." Then Markos startled him by flicking a finger and suddenly snarling Zephan in a whipping rope of pure white. If there was a reasonable amount of fear on Zephan's face before, it was nothing like the wide-eyed look he had now.

"What in magic—" Zephan bared his teeth. "Dragon prince! Rein in your angel pet and his tricks." He struggled against the glowing white bindings, and blue fae magic crackled along his skin, but Leksander could scent the fear on him. A light sheen of sweat broke out on Zephan's face.

Leksander unsheathed his blade and stepped toward the fae, but Markos's booming voice, just a notch below angelsong, made him hesitate. "What is your purpose here?" the angel demanded of Zephan with the voice of a god ringing through the throne room. "The *Truth*, fae prince. Or I'll force it from your lips. And that will not be pleasant."

Zephan quailed now—literally shaking within his restraints—and his face twisted like he was in pain or about to cry.

Leksander just stared at him, mesmerized by the torment.

"You angels and your vapid love of humans!" he spat. "Even Elyon is obsessed with them. If you had an ounce of sense, you'd be on my side! You'd see what a disease they are. A plague on the earth!"

Markos advanced on Zephan so quickly that Leksander had to step back. "What is your intent with them, fae?" The angel's booming voice hurt Leksander's ears.

He flicked a look to his brothers—everyone in the room was on high alert. Maybe Leksander wouldn't have to kill Zephan after all. Markos might do it himself. You do *not* fuck around with threatening humanity—not with an angel.

"Humans." Zephan gritted his teeth as if the word caused him pain. "They're like a virus that keeps spreading and mutating and getting stronger. They're a threat to every immortal in all the realms, and you fucking angels can't see beyond your infatuation with them." His face twisted more. Was Markos doing something to the fae? Or was admitting the unvarnished truth just causing Zephan that much pain? "You *idiots*. Do you even pay attention to what they're doing? They're mastering too much quantum science. They're unpacking the secrets of the magical realms. But they're still weak. *Now* is the time to stop them."

"Stop them how?" Markos's words shook the walls of the throne room. "Tell me, fae, if you value your life."

Zephan struggled against his angelic bindings, and he roared out when he got nowhere with that. Then he glared at Markos with bared teeth, and actual tears leaked from the corners of his eyes. *"The demons,"* he gasped as if the words were physically pulled from him. "It brings out the humans' inherent evil—you angels are so blind! You think humans are angels-in-disguise, but you're blind to their true nature. They are made of demon! You think they are especially loved by your God, but look at them! They are pathetic. They do not deserve to be the top species on the planet! Seattle is just a testing ground. And my work is a wonder to behold. They're tearing themselves apart!" Zephan's arrogance was rearing up again. "Eliminating the protection of the House of Smoke would have made all this much simpler. Breaking the treaty was the *easy* path! But by no means necessary. It doesn't violate the treaty to let humanity destroy itself." He lifted his chin defiantly to Markos. "Tapping humanity's demon essence has *always* been the plan. They *will* destroy themselves. And you can thank me later, *angel*, for saving the immortal realms from them."

The fury on Markos's face thrummed power throughout the room. "You will *stop* this demon infection. Now."

"No." A mad glimmer shone in Zephan's eyes. "I won't. And neither will you. Not as long as Elyon and his forces outnumber you ten to one." The glimmer crept into a twisted smirk. "You have no choice, light angel. You *need* me. Stop Elyon *now*... before he destroys everything. Then we can discuss how to keep the humans contained to the mortal realm. Because you know it, angel—*you know*, no matter how you pretend otherwise!—that the humans, if they gain access to magic, will be a curse on heaven as much as on earth!" Zephan's chest heaved, and his lips trembled, but there was no doubt in Leksander's mind. *He was telling the truth.*

Holy shit.

Leksander waited for Markos to respond. The angel's face was livid with righteous anger, and Leksander honestly didn't know if he would simply smite Zephan or if Markos would do as the fae said and take the fight outside the keep. Either would work.

Because despite Zephan's insistence that they needed him to save humanity, Leksander would put a blade in the fae, if Markos didn't do it first.

The towering angel wavered… then stepped back from Zephan.

It was as if the fae had ceased to exist. Markos turned to Leksander. "You must drop the wards and allow us to face Elyon. We will defeat him, even if I have to call in Warrior Angels and their brethren. Then the demon scourge can be easily handled. And with your treaty renewed, humanity will once again be safe from the fae."

"Sounds like a plan," Leksander said, lifting his chin to Leonidas. He was all for Markos taking on Elyon. And nothing in Markos's plan said Leksander couldn't bury a blade in Zephan as soon as Markos was outside the keep.

The angel circled his hand, and his two dozen angelings tensed, all apparently ready to transport as soon as the wards were down. It only took a moment. Leonidas dropped the wards, Markos and his cohort disappeared, and the wards went back up. Zephan was trapped inside Markos's bindings—even if he wanted to leave, he couldn't. But now he had his wish… Markos outside, protecting his sorry ass from Elyon, the shadow angel whose insanity Zephan had unleased.

Just one more reason Zephan deserved to die.

Leksander lurched forward, yanking his angel blade from its sheath and raising his hand for the strike.

Zephan's eyes flew wide. *"No!"* he cried out, struggling against his bonds.

Leksander aimed for the heart, but a blast of energy picked up Zephan, threw him into Leksander's blade, then tossed them both across the room. Leksander roared in frustration and shoved Zephan's body off him. His angel blade stuck out of the fae's chest—it hadn't run true through his heart, but it was buried deep, and the fae's thick, blue-magic blood was surging out of his chest and his mouth. His face was stricken, and Leksander figured the wound had to be fatal. Or nearly so. But making sure was definitely called for. He reached to yank the blade out and strike again, but a force gripped Leksander and threw him against a wall, stunning him so badly that he saw double.

Only then did he realize that something had gone terribly, terribly wrong.

Leonidas and Lucian lay crumpled on the floor by the throne... a throne where Tajael had been slumped but which was now empty. In his place stood an oversized angel with terrifying dark eyes and long white hair that flared out in a magical wind.

Malevolence was writ on his face.

Elyon.

The shadow angel flicked a hand at Leksander, and everything went black.

Chapter Fifteen

THE WAITING WOULD KILL HER.

Erelah paced the small confines of the guest room. She was on her hundredth circuit already—another would drive her mad. And besides, she was becoming dizzy. The tight circles she was walking in the small room? Or faintness from the lack of food she couldn't bear to eat?

She would give a few blood feathers to have Leksander return.

She trusted him. She believed his True Love would return him to her if such a thing were possible. But she had to keep reassuring herself that he still lived by bringing a hand near the wall of the guest room. It pulsed with his magic, crackling with a blue-magic static feedback whenever she came close to touching it. She cupped her hands under her belly instead.

"It is your time, little one," she whispered to the baby. "But wait until your daddy returns."

The baby hummed a little angelsong, just a small trill, in response. She loved him like no other human soul on earth, save Leksander's. Each kick, each song, each little wiggle, yearning to be free was a delight to her heart. She wondered if she might feel differently once he was born—after all, he was part of her now. Soon, he would be his own separate, little being. She could already feel the loss of him. But no… it would be a gain in so many ways. A first breath. A new life. A treaty renewed.

Peace.

Her son deserved to grow up in peace just as Rachel's child and Rosalyn's and Arabella's. The love of dragons and humans, long a mystery to her, now seemed like the fabric of the universe—it had always been and would always be, and it tied everything together. It filled the House of Smoke with magic, and it was wrong for anything to threaten those True Loves, much less destroy them, as the forces of shadow and fae had been trying to do.

Her son deserved nothing but love… and she would ensure it with her life.

The baby fluttered inside her. More than just a simple kick, this was a whole shifting around. A movement that made her wonder if he had wings in her womb. And would they be dragon or angel? The discomfort grew enough that she had to stand if only to give the child more room. Her angel blade lay on the table against the wall, so she walked over to grab it, just to have something to do. She paced the floor again, flipping her blade between forward and reverse grips.

The pain of childbirth would be upon her soon. She knew this but did not fear it. Her tolerance for Penance was high, and besides, her angel nature would quickly heal whatever damage might be done in easing the child from her body. She feared more for the baby than herself.

The child shifted again, causing her to pause in her circuit. He seemed to have dropped lower somehow, so perhaps that was what he sought—a settling spot in her womb. Which quieted him, but now her walking was slower and clumsier. She waddled slowly across the room, rocking the baby as she went. It seemed awkward to walk, but she couldn't imagine sitting in this state. She paused at a small dresser tucked to the side of the room, and for no reason other than her body seemed most at comfort standing, she opened the drawers, one by one. It momentarily eased the tension of the wait. The first was empty, and the second contained only a blanket, but the third…

A glowing white box sat in the corner, humming with angel power.

She knew exactly what it was—*a blessing*. The one Markos had gifted to Leksander for his child and his mate, long before Erelah had any sense *she* would be the one to carry his baby. And how fortunate for her to have found it!

She set down her blade and scooped the blessing box out of the drawer. It hummed in her hand, and she immediately sensed it was meant for her. Or more accurately, for the baby. She pressed the box to her belly, and the blessing sought the child within. But she and the baby were *one*… and so the life boost flowed through her as well, radiating out from her belly and filling every particle of her being with light and love and life.

She gasped in a breath with the joy it brought.

Then she gasped for a different reason—a pain chased after the joy, spreading in its wake like a river that floods and crests its banks.

The box clattered to the floor.

She clutched at her belly, for it suddenly felt as if it were pulling apart. The pain surged and spread, a wave once more bursting its restraints and passing through her body, front to back. She braced against the drawers, for the dizziness was back, and the baby seemed to shift even lower in her belly. Then a hot gush of liquid came forth from her, sliding down her legs and dashing to the floor. She stared down in horror, relieved to see no blood, only water.

Then she remembered. When she had freed Rosalyn's baby of the demon, taking it with her blade, he had been badly weakened by the struggle. So she gave him a life kiss straight through her belly—a magic infusion of life. But then... the labor began. Literally, the instant the life kiss had finished, the baby began to depart his mother's body —to begin his life, ready and strong and brimming with vitality. *The blessing box...* the same angel magic as a life kiss...

Her baby was coming.

"No, no, baby," she panted. "You need to wait for your daddy." But a wave of pain wracked her again, making her curl over her belly, and she knew it was useless. This baby was coming *now.*

She grabbed her angel blade and stumbled away from the dresser, lurching to the bed. But then the baby shifted even lower, and an incredible pressure started as if the baby were *pushing...* trying to work his way out...

She grasped hold of the bed and roughly sat down on the edge, setting the blade near the pillows. Then she pulsed magic to the screen on the wall, the one she could use to call Rosalyn. It took her three tries as the baby's birthing pains made her cry out and double over—and she nearly shook the screen from the wall—but finally, Rosalyn's concerned face filled it.

"The baby!" Erelah gasped. "He is coming." Her voice was raw and breathy, and she could barely get the words out.

"Oh, shit!" Rosalyn grimaced and ran off the screen.

Erelah had no idea where she planned to go, but

another birthing pain wracked her—this one nearly sent her to the floor, so she forced herself to crawl up onto the bed. She couldn't risk falling, not while in this state. It was a long, breathy struggle, but she made it to the head of the bed, where it met the wall. She managed to heave herself into a somewhat upright sitting position. She cried out again when a birthing pain gripped her—*angels of light, it felt as if she were coming apart*—but when it eased, the pressure down low in her belly remained, constant and forceful.

"Erelah!" It was Rosalyn. She had returned to the screen.

Erelah squinted at her. Sweat was drenching her brow and dripping into her eyes, and it seemed as if Rosalyn had become two people. Erelah had to clear her vision, then she saw Rachel had joined Rosalyn in the view of the screen, and the background had shifted to a couch where Rachel was likewise propped up with a similar sweat-drenched face.

"Okay, you two!" Rosalyn was saying, both to Erelah and Rachel. "Apparently, we're having these babies at the same time! Now push!"

"Push?" Erelah asked. "Push what?" But her whispered question was drowned out by Rachel's litany of curses, many of which Erelah did not understand, but she intuited their meaning. And then Rachel's cursing became one long scream as she hunched over her belly, knees spread and gripped in her hands… and Erelah understood.

She had to push the baby out.

The thought sent another wave of dizziness through her.

"Breathe!" Rosalyn shouted at Rachel. The woman's face was turning red with effort.

Erelah tried breathing herself—longer, deep breaths—

but then the pain wracked her again, and she was one, giant, curled up ball. A long drop of sweat dripped from her nose before the pain receded. Then she leaned back and rested her head against the wall.

The electric buzz of the wards made her quickly lift her head again. But just as she was giving a prayer of thanks—live wards meant Leksander was still alive—the magic crackled and pulsed right behind her. She leaned forward and looked back at it.

"What was that?" Rosalyn asked. But it was clear she wasn't asking Erelah—her gaze was casting about her own lair.

"I do not—" The sound of electric buzzing cut Erelah off—it sounded as if... as if the wards themselves were shorting out! Her eyes flew wide.

"Holy shit," Rosalyn breathed. Her gaze met Erelah's. "Someone's trying to break the wards."

"No." It was a whisper of breath, but it was all she got out before the pain gripped her again. As she curled up over her stomach—*her baby*—one thought blazed through her mind, cutting through the pain and the static hum and the electric snapping of the wards.

Now.

Now, little one.

It's time.

Erelah grabbed hold of her knees as Rachel had... *and pushed.*

Chapter Sixteen

Leksander was being dragged.

As he swam up into consciousness, the first thing he saw was his own boots scraping along the floor of the hallway. *A hallway in the keep.* Something had him by the back of the neck with a fiery-hot grip, and he couldn't move at all —just submit to being hauled down the corridor.

Elyon.

The memory rushed back, making him jolt. He could see the back of the shadow angel's leather body armor as they bumped down the hallway. Leksander twisted and fought his hold, but that just earned him a smack against the wall that jarred his brain so hard he fell limp again.

"Cooperate, and I might not kill you." Elyon's voice boomed down the empty hall behind them.

Fuck. Leksander would give his life to stop this asshole, but that was precisely what he couldn't do. The death wards were the only thing protecting Erelah now. Leksander cursed himself silently in dragontongue. The ancient words for *fucking idiot* were ready on his tongue. *How could he be so foolish?* He knew angels could take any form they liked, but somehow Elyon pretending to be Tajael completely fooled him. He even *tasted* the shadow angel on Tajael, but Leksander just figured the angeling was struggling with his nature, as Erelah had.

It even fooled Markos.

Who was now outside the keep.

That was what he needed. *Help.* Leksander reached out to pull down the wards—the grip on his neck tightened, and suddenly, it was made of *fire.* Leksander screamed as the burning tore through him, not just where Elyon held him but ripping like a wildfire through the magic in his veins. Then he was slammed into the wall again, blanking out the pain with the stunning force of it.

"It is not *those* wards I wish you to bring down, beast." Elyon hauled him up to standing, which Leksander could barely do—his legs still shook from the knock on the head and the burning torture magic. Only then did Leksander realize exactly where they were.

Right outside his lair.

Goddammit. That meant Elyon had already broken through the wards around this half of the keep—the wards that protected all three lairs of the princes of the House of Smoke. And their mates. And dragonlings. Did Elyon know that? He certainly knew where to come to get Erelah, even though she was behind the wards, and he couldn't possibly sense her. Leksander prayed the angel had left the others alone, coming straight here.

"How about you fuck off?" he said, hopefully distracting Elyon while he shot his fae senses out again to bring down the outside wards—before he could, Elyon held up his palm, and that murderous pain struck Leksander down once more. He couldn't help the screams or sinking to his knees. *He was on fire.* That was the only thought he could manage through the torment.

Then it cut off again, just as quickly, leaving him breathless.

"Too bad you've sided with the light," Elyon mused. "At the Great Fall, your kind and mine were natural allies."

"Fuck. You." Leksander gasped, trying to struggle up from the floor. What the fuck was happening here? He tried to fight through the leftover haze in his mind. Elyon could easily kill him. But he hadn't. Because he wanted Leksander to bring down the wards—not the ones around the keep, which would let Markos back in. And not the common wards around the lairs. Elyon had already broken those. But Elyon couldn't break the death wards around his lair. He might not even *know* they were death wards.

He needed Leksander's help.

Elyon magically lifted Leksander up, but not to standing—he jerked Leksander up off the ground and flung him against the door of his own lair. The door protected by his own death wards. The magic burned and sizzled across his back and his scalp. He roared against the pain. After long seconds of agony—Leksander felt sure his brain was being electrocuted—Elyon released him.

He slumped once more to the floor.

This time he stayed down.

"A clever ward," Elyon said. His voice was laced with danger. "Its strength is an unexpected inconvenience. Bring it down."

Leksander didn't bother answering. No matter what, he had to stay alive. His death was the only way to break the wards, and as long as Elyon didn't know that—

The hellfire in his veins surged up. Leksander couldn't help the way his body twitched and rolled as if instinctively trying to put out a fire made of magic the way you might with actual flames. His screams rasped his throat, and when the pain stopped this time, he was lying on his back, staring up at Elyon's face. His black eyes and wild white hair marred his perfect beauty. Leksander stared dully at him, his tongue thick. It seemed strange that something so perfectly evil could be contained in that angelic form… although that just reminded him this was the form Elyon *chose*.

"I *will* kill you," Elyon said with a small smile. "And your mate will perish, too."

"No," Leksander answered thickly, unable to muster even a proper *Fuck off, you fucking evil bastard angel.* He stayed on the floor. He wasn't sure his limbs would work right anyway.

"The fae was right." Elyon curled a lip, revealing perfectly white teeth. "Humans are a pestilence better wiped from the earth. Breaking the treaty will allow the Winter Court to do just that. But even if that weren't true, this halfling you've spawned must die. If I'd reached your mate sooner, I might have simply turned her or taken the baby for myself. But the time for such things is past. Other-wise, the angels of light might think they can rule the shadow. Or even eliminate us once and for all." Elyon reached down to grab Leksander by the throat and hauled him off the floor.

All his air cut off. He clawed at Elyon's hand, but it was like being choked by a god. Elyon pulled him closer until they were face-to-face. Leksander was far from small, but this oversized angel had his feet pawing the air—air he couldn't pull into his lungs.

"I have endless ways to torment you, dragon." His smile gleamed. "And if I can't break your mind with pain, I will do it with pleasure—either way, I will have what I seek."

Black stars swam in front of Leksander's eyes… *he was passing out.* But that was fine. Torment was fine. All of it, he would endure… as long as Elyon didn't kill him. And at some small moment—just an instant of time when Elyon was distracted was all he needed—Leksander would bring down the outside wards and bring help.

Elyon's eyes narrowed at Leksander's lack of response. Did he expect more of a struggle? Then the angel flicked a look past Leksander's shoulder at the door to his lair and the invisible wards protecting it.

"These wards are different." The angel's voice was dangerously thoughtful. Then he tossed Leksander against the wall of this lair. The electric shock of it jolted him again, but he was only in contact for an instant. He crashed to the floor, gasping in the air he'd been fighting for. Elyon was back to staring at the door, and a cold flush of fear ran through Leksander. "The others weren't so hard to break," Elyon said, still staring at the door. "A simple trick and a surge of power. But those tasted of common magic. Dragon magic. These taste of… *fae.*" He turned a narrow-eyed glare at Leksander. "Of your useless True Love. And of *death.*" His eyes widened.

Holy shit. Leksander roared, spewing dragonfire and shifting into his dragon as he hurled himself at the angel. Talons, needle-sharp fangs, and the shock of surprise—all of it was his for an instant. If Elyon was going to kill him, Leksander would make sure the outer wards came down first. As he attacked, slashing and biting and clinging despite Elyon reeling back and lashing out, Leksander screamed—*in dragontongue*—the ancient words of his House, finally bringing down the wards around the keep.

The last word got out. The wards came down. And Elyon blasted him with a pulse that felt like it ripped him in two.

Leksander tumbled down the hall, reflexively shifting human again as his mind screamed in pain. When he stopped, the pain kept on. Plus something buffeted against him, rolling him further down the hall. Magic. Some hellaciously strong magic was sweeping pulses down the hall. He fought through the pain and the magical tide and tried to rise up from the floor, but he kept slipping on something. Everywhere was wet—his hands, his legs.

It took a moment to realize… *it was his blood.*

Smeared across the floor like a macabre surrealist painting. Drenching his clothes as if he were losing it by the gallon. He clutched his gut through the slashes in his blood-soaked shirt—that ripped a fire of pain through him —and he managed to fight the slippery floor enough to slide into sitting propped against the wall.

And then all energy escaped him. He had to fight to remain conscious.

He half expected Elyon to come after him to finish the job.

But when Leksander blinked away the haze of pain and the lightheaded feeling—*fuck*, he was losing so much blood, magical blood, too much blood—he saw why Elyon hadn't *already* killed him.

The hall was filled with angelings. A flurry of feathers and blades and singing angel power so intense, Leksander almost couldn't tell one from the other, light from shadow. And the waves of magic kept pulsing through the hall, adding to the chaos, crashing one against another. An angeling of light with his back to Leksander screamed a warrior cry and slashed his blade through the air. Its arc buried in the chest of the shadow angeling charging him.

Then the angeling of light turned on Leksander. "Are you all right, dragon prince?"

It was Tajael.

Leksander laughed, but the sound was choked and made his chest scream with pain. Drool leaked from his mouth, so he wiped it… then he stared at the back of his hand, which was smeared with blood. He blinked wearily up at the stricken expression on Tajael's face.

"Don't… don't let me die." Leksander's words were garbled. The blood coated his mouth and tasted of iron.

Tajael whirled and slashed at another attacking shadow angeling, and in that brief moment, Leksander saw through the melee of feathers both light and shadow to the power struggle happening further down the hall. Elyon was grappling with Markos… and another angel. A shadow angel. *Razael.* Erelah's father had returned. It appeared he was fighting by Markos's side—light joined with shadow—slowly beating Elyon back, farther away from Leksander and his lair. A new pulse of angel energy surged with each clash, but Markos and Razael had formed a wall of angel power that relentlessly pushed Elyon back.

"Leksander!" Tajael grabbed his attention… and his shoulder. Then he swept out behind him with his blade, wrenching Leksander as well. He screamed his pain… only they weren't in the hallway anymore.

They were in the throne room.

"Did you fare well the trip?" Tajael asked hastily, bent at his side, scanning Leksander's body with his gaze. Leksander couldn't see his own wounds through the mess of blood and tattered shirt, but he knew it was dire. He could *feel* the death stealing over him, haunting him. Or maybe it was just the loss of blood. But as long as they were back in the throne room…

"Where's Zephan?" Leksander might die soon—he had to live long enough to keep the death wards up, until the baby was born—but he would make sure Zephan left this world before him.

"Zephan?" Tajael was confused. "He was the one who held me. Then he brought Elyon, so he could create a glamour of me, and I knew this wouldn't end well. They left, and I broke free—"

Leksander had no time for this. He stopped listening and twisted to look for Zephan in the now-empty throne room. *There.* The fae was still slumped against the wall, an angel blade sticking out of his chest.

Tajael followed his gaze, then his eyes went wide as he took in Zephan's state. The blue blood had spread across his chest. Not as much as Leksander had already lost, but the fae prince's face was even more unnaturally pale, and his eyes were closed.

"Is he dead?" Leksander asked.

"I think not," Tajael said with a frown. "Fae do not possess souls the way humans do, but—"

"Tajael." He had to grab hold of the angeling's arm just to stay sitting upright.

"I will not leave your side." Tajael scowled.

Leksander groaned and attempted to rise up from sitting. All he could manage was to crawl on hands and knees, which meant letting go of his gut. He was pretty sure his insides would fall out if he did, and he couldn't afford to die. Not yet. So with one hand gripping his stomach, he crawled toward Zephan's inert body.

"Dragon prince!" Tajael was in a panic. "What are you doing?"

Leksander didn't respond. He saved his energy for the crawl.

"Stop!" Tajael leaped to stand in his way. "For the love of magic, stay here! I will bring the fae to you."

Leksander wearily nodded, once, then settled to the floor again. Tajael ran across the twenty feet of throne room separating Leksander and the fallen fae. But just as he reached Zephan's body, a flash of light and a pop of the air announced the arrival of another immortal.

A dark-haired fae appeared at Zephan's side. He roared with anger and blasted Tajael aside. The angeling flew backward, crashing into the wall of the throne room. Then the fae turned to face Leksander—it was a male with a haughty face full of anger. *Remasay, King of the Winter Court.* Zephan's father.

He raised a hand in Leksander's direction.

Suddenly, a woman with flying white hair appeared between them. The fae king's magic blasted against her, but she returned the magical pulse with equal power, rocking the king back on his heels. By that time, Tajael had recovered. He charged forward, blade raised.

The woman cried out, "Stop!" but before Tajael could reach them, the king stooped to Zephan's side, laid a hand on him, and twisted away.

Both Zephan and his father were gone in another flash of interdimensional magic.

Tajael stumbled to a stop then turned his blade on the woman. She sent him reeling with another blast of fae power, and only then did she turn to face Leksander…

Nyssa, Queen of the Summer Court. Daughter of the original fae queen who was his grandmother ten generations removed. The fae he almost bedded in desperation when he felt sure Erelah would never love him. Violet eyes, snow-white endlessly long hair… and his apparent savior today.

Tajael looked confused—and more than a little wary. He hurried back to Leksander's side, keeping his blade pointed at Nyssa.

"She's a friend," Leksander gasped out. Then he peered at Nyssa. "Right?" The last time he'd seen her, they parted on good terms. But still. With the fae, you never knew.

She strolled forward. "My court has been monitoring your situation, Leksander. You've managed to rile the entire immortal world." She didn't sound entirely disapproving.

"It's a talent," he ground out. His head swam, and he had to blink away the black stars again.

Tajael urged him to lean back to the floor. "You must let me heal you."

Leksander had no energy to resist. He laid down, grimacing as he went.

Nyssa moved closer, hovering over him with a worried look.

Leksander gripped Tajael's arm. "Tell me Zephan was dead."

"I didn't have time to tell." The angeling was peeling off the bloody shreds of Leksander's shirt. If Leksander could lift his head to look, he wouldn't be surprised to see his midsection half sliced away. The expression on Tajael's face told him all he needed to know.

He wasn't going to make it.

Leksander grabbed Tajael's wrist to stop him, but it was so weak, the angeling could have easily continued. He didn't. "Tell me," Leksander gasped. There was a horrible rattle in his voice now. "Tell me I killed him."

Tajael looked pained. Leksander couldn't tell if it was his wound or the desperation in his voice. "A fae's magic lingers on after death—"

"Tajael."

The angeling winced and looked to Nyssa.

She scowled. "Zephan left here alive. But he may not be for much longer."

Tajael laid his hands flat on Leksander's bloody chest. "And neither will you if you don't let me tend to you."

"Fuck." But the word made Leksander cough, and he could feel the blood leaking from the corner of his mouth again. How he had any left, he had no idea.

Tajael bent over him and breathed on the bloody tatters of Leksander's chest. Leksander tipped his head back, the life kiss from Tajael infusing him with energy and easing the horrible throb of the pain, just a little... but even he could tell it wasn't enough.

He gripped Tajael's wrist to stop him. "She'll need you," Leksander rasped. He didn't want Tajael giving away all his life energy when Erelah and the baby would need *someone* after he was gone.

"You're not going to die," Tajael said, angrily. Too angry. Which meant Leksander absolutely would die.

"You've lost too much blood," Nyssa said, anger filling her voice as well.

"Sorry." Leksander's head was swimming. Everyone was angry at him as if dying was part of his plan. The dizziness got worse, and he needed to tell them... "Can't die. Death wards. Tajael... death wards... protecting Erelah." The words were all jumbled in his mouth now. He tried and failed to grasp at Tajael's arm, but he wasn't seeing straight anymore. It seemed like the room was spinning. Tajael going clockwise, and Nyssa going counter-clockwise. Which made no sense. And their mouths were moving, but the sound was disjointed. Out of sync. Out of time.

He was out of time.

"Step aside."

"You'll not harm him."

"Don't be an idiot. He's my cousin."

"That means nothing."

"Do you want him to die? Step aside."

They were words, but Leksander couldn't attach meaning to them. Like they were floating in the whirlpool of air that was thick and pressing down on his chest. Then, suddenly, the whirlpool lifted, and more of that life kiss flooded into him—a sizzling kind of magic laced with the effervescence of life. But there was something more to it… something familiar…

Fae. Angel power mixed with fae magic.

It was pumping serious energy into him now, chasing away the stench of death creeping up on him. His head cleared, and the dizziness stopped. He pulled in a huge breath of air—as if his lungs were suddenly functioning again—and sensation flooded back into his body. He blinked his eyes clear.

Both Nyssa and Tajael were bent over him, one on each side.

Tajael's hands were spread across his chest, and Leksander could feel the healing happen as his grievous wounds stitched themselves back together. Nyssa's silky white dress was drenched in his blood. As he watched, she took a dagger she must have conjured and slashed across her wrist and held it to his wounds… she wasn't just using fae magic to heal him. She was literally donating fae-magic-filled blood. She was restoring what he lost… or at least enough that his natural dragon blood could recover and start to restore his normal blood volume.

Remarkably, after a minute of this, he felt well enough to sit up.

Or try to.

Tajael shoved him back down. "Don't make me regret this, dragon prince." He looked haggard, cheeks hollow, eyes sunken. Like when he'd almost "given too much" to Erelah to save her from her own near-miss with death.

Leksander dutifully laid back down but still peered at Nyssa. "Cousin, huh?"

She gave him a look of disgust. "Well, you have half my blood now, so I guess that makes us blood relatives."

He grinned. "You have a soft spot for dragons."

She gave a sigh. "You're seriously more trouble than you're worth."

He shook his head, confused. "Why, Nyssa?"

"For starters, because you've caused an immortal war—"

"No." Leksander struggled again to sit up, but this time Tajael helped him, apparently satisfied that all his parts were sufficiently healed. "I mean, why bother to save me?" He probed his chest among the tatters of his bloodied shirt. Shockingly, he had no more open wounds. The power of fae and angel healing combined was impressive.

"You must renew the treaty, Leksander," Nyssa said like this was obvious. "We cannot have a war between Winter and Summer amidst all this..." She gestured to the keep around them. *"Chaos."*

Tajael was still looking him over. "Erelah will have the child without you. You need to stay here where you're safe in order to ensure her safety."

The death wards. Leksander reached out with his fae senses, sensing what Nyssa and Tajael both must have already. The common wards were still down—around the keep and around the lairs. Only Leksander's death wards held. A melee of angelings was still thrashing near the door to Leksander's lair, but Markos and Razael had successfully moved Elyon to the far edge of the rambling keep. But they were still here.

The battle had yet to be won.

"Tajael's right." Leksander grimaced. "I can't bring down the wards until the angels and angelings are done with their fighting."

Nyssa planted her hands on her hips. "Conjure a ward to contain them."

Leksander peered at her. "Elyon already broke the

common wards. Another death ward would be too dangerous."

"It doesn't have to hold for long," Nyssa argued. "Just long enough for you to lower and raise that death ward which you so foolishly and brilliantly set for your True Love. I will have your back, prince of the House of Smoke. No angel will get easily past me *and* an immortal ward."

Leksander flicked a look to Tajael.

"It should work," he said with a frown. "But I don't like it. What is the urgency? You can simply wait it out."

"Simply wait it out," Nyssa mocked him. To Leksander, she said, "If I were the one bearing your child, dragon prince, I would want you by my side. Nay, my heart would break to not have you there. And if there is a thing that your particular flavor of mating requires…"

"It's True Love." Leksander's heart quickened. "I need to be there, Tajael. Erelah needs to know my love to make it all the way through this. To see it to the end."

"She does not doubt you, dragon prince!" His face was filled with disbelief. "Your love has been her constant in all this."

"Exactly why I need to be there now." Leksander made it to his feet without too much difficulty. He marveled at the fact that he was breathing at all.

Nyssa nodded her approval. "Even your common wards have the power of righteousness in them. They're defensive spells. Your unique gift as dragons, protectors of these soft and rather pathetic creatures."

"You mean the humans," Leksander said with a smirk. "I'm mated to an *angeling*."

Her lips drew back in a snarl. "Don't remind me. I choose to forget that part." She threw a look of disgust at Tajael, who seemed likewise not the least enamored with her.

She held out her hand to Leksander. "Shall we?"

"I'm coming as well," Tajael said, frowning like he thought Nyssa might steal him away.

"Surprise is our friend," Leksander said to them both. "Get me to the door of my lair. I'll throw up a personal ward sealing us in, at least momentarily. Then I'll slip inside. I'm depending on you, Nyssa, to hold the angelings back." He grabbed hold of her hand at the same time Tajael placed his hand on Leksander's shoulder.

The three of them twisted, all at once, and the throne room disappeared.

Suddenly, they were at his lair, in the middle of a fight that was even bloodier than when he left. Half the angelings—both shadow and light—were lying on the floor, dead or horrifically wounded. The others were climbing the walls, flying, boosting off every available surface, a tight acrobatics of combat that had angel blades flashing all over the hall. Leksander threw up a personal ward around him and Tajael, purposely leaving Nyssa out of the scope so she could use her magic. He and Tajael stood back-to-back as Leksander worked to carefully bring down the death ward he had so earnestly placed. It didn't take long—just a few seconds—but in that time, Nyssa conjured what looked like a hundred enormous white butterflies. *Her sprites.* They fluttered off into the melee, crashing and bursting upon angelings indiscriminately. They started falling from the air, and Leksander feared they might be dead.

He couldn't worry about that.

The death ward was down. He quickly hurried inside his lair, giving a nod to Tajael who stood guard outside. Nyssa was already walking amongst the carnage in the hall, making sure every last angeling met its match in a sprite.

Leksander closed the door, his heart pounding, and raised the death ward once more. Then he raced to the guest room and went through the whole dance again. As he was bringing the death ward down, he heard a scream inside that made him go cold down to his bones. He finished unraveling the ward and yanked open the door—

An angel blade sailed through the air and embedded in the doorframe next to his head.

"Whoa!" He stepped back through the still open door. "It's just—" But then his beloved cried out again, and he raced to Erelah's side. There was no way she would have missed him if she weren't in the greatest of pain. "I'm here," he said, falling to his knees by the bedside. *Sweet magic,* she was drenched in sweat, curled up over her belly, gripping her knees. Her face was contorted with pain. "Angel girl, I'm here." He slipped a hand to the back of her neck to support her, and another to her legs to ease the tension.

Only then did she seem to recognize his presence. Her eyes flew wide, and her face lit with joy. But then the pain gripped her face, twisting it again, and she screamed and groaned her way through another contraction.

"I'm here, my love. I'm here." He just kept saying it over and over, petting her and holding her and supporting her any way he could.

When the pain released her, she panted like she could barely catch her breath. "You… You made it. You're back. I knew… I knew you'd come back."

"Of course." He fought to keep the surge of emotion from overwhelming him.

She laid her hand on his, the one holding up her knee. "If I have you… all things are possible."

Words caught in his throat, and he couldn't speak. *At*

all. But that didn't matter because the pain was gripping her again.

She screamed and groaned and then said, "The baby! He's coming!" And with a final, long, groaning push… his child slipped into the world. Leksander had to let her go to reach for the baby, and then when he eased the tiny, precious bundle fully from his mother's body, the wonder of it almost made him cry out.

Erelah *did* cry out—in relief—then she gasped in air and fell back on the bed.

"Erelah!" His gaze jerked up to her. "Are you okay?" He carefully cradled the baby to his chest.

She lifted her head to peer between her still-splayed legs, but a smile was on her face. "We have a child."

He thought he might burst with happiness.

Then a *boom* shook the walls. His heart seized. *No, no, no…* He flung his fae senses out, but the wards were still in place. Relief escaped him in one long huff. He was *inside* the wards now. They could only be breached by his death… and he was not going to die. Not anymore.

They were *safe.*

Truly safe. All three of them.

And when he looked to Erelah… she was smiling.

"It's the magic." Already her voice was returning to normal.

"What magic?" he asked, thoroughly confused. With his hands full of baby, he couldn't really do anything but settle on the bed at her feet as she worked her way up to sitting.

"The magic of the treaty."

The magic of the treaty. It struck him hard, almost like a second boom through magical space. "We did it." His grin grew slowly, then faster, then it took over his face entirely. "We renewed the treaty."

Her smile radiated joy. *"He* renewed the treaty," she said, reaching for the baby. Then her smile dimmed, and a strange look of wonder took over her face.

"What's wrong?" Leksander asked, panic seizing his heart for the second time in a dozen seconds. His gaze swept the baby. Those big eyes blinking and looking up at him. Tiny, perfect hands curled up under his chin. He was moving, breathing, pinking up in color, and…

Holy mother of magic.

Leksander looked up at the angeling he loved. "Our baby is a girl!"

The smile was back on Erelah's face. "Of course, she is. She's my angeling after all."

A huff of surprise and sheer, blinding relief tore through him.

A girl dragonling in the House of Smoke.

A treaty renewed.

And everything he could possibly want in life in one tiny bed in the guest room of his lair.

He laughed with the joy of it, and tears slipped down his face that he didn't bother wiping away. He just handed his baby girl over to her momma then wrapped his arms around them both.

He didn't know if he deserved this joy, but he didn't care.

He had it. And he was never letting go.

Chapter Seventeen

"A female," cooed the fae queen. "About time you had a female fae in this House."

"She's a dragonling," Leksander answered. Erelah could hear the growl in his voice as he cuddled their daughter closer.

"Obviously, the angeling is strongest in her," Erelah said. "You will see, when her wings appear." Could they not taste the angel in her baby? She could allow Leksander's desire to believe their daughter was dragon—and clearly, she was dragon *enough* to fulfill the treaty; that was an indisputable magical fact—but Erelah knew *the Truth.*

Her child was an angeling of the light who would change the world.

Her only hope was that it would be *for the better.*

The three of them stood in the throne room on the dais, just to one side of King Lucian and Queen Arabella, with baby Larik sleeping in the crook of the king's arm. Leonidas and Rosalyn stood on the opposite side of the throne, Leonidas's arm around Rosalyn as baby Thorn fussed quietly at her bosom, taking his morning meal. Rachel and Cinaed were guests of honor next to them. The blue dragon beamed unmistakable pride in the dragonling Rachel had borne for him, likewise sleeping in his arms.

Babies born against all odds, in a world determined to stop True Love... *and failing.*

Erelah's attention was drawn back to the fae queen paying her respects in front of them. Nyssa was her name, and while Erelah loathed all fae by nature, this one earned her forbearance. After all, her blood ran in Leksander's veins, and she had saved his life. For that, Erelah would forever owe the queen a debt of gratitude.

"Well, I approve of the name, at least," Nyssa remarked, giving a wide smile to the baby. "Aurora is so much better than one of those odd angeling names you all seem to choose." Nyssa flicked a look at Erelah, then Tajael standing by her side, opposite Leksander. "No offense."

"None taken," Tajael answered, coolly, obviously offended.

Erelah was no good at reading human social interaction, but an angeling's war with Pride? That she could see a mile away.

She restrained a laugh.

Especially given how much serious danger still lay before the world. She gazed down at her beautiful daughter, as perfect as any angeling in appearance, but equally shining in the beauty of her soul. *Aurora. A new beginning.* It was the name her father had intended for her —her *true* father, Razael, now a shadow angel, but once a brilliant angel of the light. Her faction leader and substitute father, Markos, stood further back in the throne room, allowing the fae queen to pay her respects. He had a faint air of disapproval about him. Or perhaps just caution.

For there was war afoot now between angels and fae.

And her child was both the nexus and the cause in that war.

Nyssa conjured a glittering, golden butterfly and held it out on her hand to bestow upon Aurora. The child was sleeping in Leksander's arms, and he gave the fae queen a wary look.

"For the love of magic, Leksander." The queen scowled. "Surely, you can trust me by now."

Leksander frowned but gave a small nod. In Truth, the fae queen could slay their child outright, and it would change nothing. The treaty had been renewed. The fact that Aurora could be born, and Erelah could remain in the light changed *everything* for angelkind. No matter what happened to her baby now, none of those facts—the ones compelling the world toward war and possibly, still, the End of Times—would change. Erelah would personally destroy anyone who even raised a hand to her child, but it would be a personal loss, the horror of a single family, not an act that unhinged the world.

There was a strange and comforting normalcy to that.

Erelah was now simply the mother of Aurora. The mate of Leksander. A princess of the House of Smoke. And an angeling of light. These things were immutable and would last all the days of her life... days which would now be long and fruitful and filled with love, even if the world were to fall to ruin around them.

She had her family, and they had her.

The joy of it still brought tears to her eyes whenever she thought on it.

Nyssa's golden butterfly sprite had alit on little Aurora's tightly curled hand. For a moment, it just flapped its wings, but then in a wink, it dissolved and sprinkled golden dust down upon her daughter, making her stir in Leksander's arms and slowly open her brilliant blue eyes. She gazed up at her daddy and hummed a bit of angelsong. The look on Leksander's face loosened those tears clinging to the corner of Erelah's eyes.

She ducked her head to wipe them away.

The entire assemblage of the throne room—dragons and angelkind alike—seemed to hold their breath, but Erelah had already sensed the sprite's purpose and knew it would pose no harm to her child.

Nyssa spoke it aloud. "It's a simple protection sprite. And it would appear your daughter will need it."

"She will have the protection of an entire Dominion of angelings," Tajael answered, tightly.

Again, Erelah had to restrain the laugh that came with that.

As well she should. There was war brewing, and not just between light and shadow, although there for certain. Her father, Razael, and her substitute father, Markos, had joined forces to defend her and her child. They had beaten back Elyon long enough, and once it was known that the child lived, Elyon had taken his surviving shadow angelings and vanished. But no one—not even Erelah—entertained any delusions he would stay hidden. Elyon would see Aurora as a *greater* threat now that she lived. He would not come after her daughter—there was no point in harming the child other than petty revenge, which in Truth, Elyon was capable of—but he was certain to be making plans for a war against the light.

Although, it was uncertain exactly where the battle lines would be drawn.

We are not friends, Markos, her father, Razael, had said, just before he kissed his granddaughter and disappeared back into the shadow. It was Truth, and Erelah was strangely proud of the shadow angel for speaking it. There had been much loss—many angeling deaths—and there would be more to come. The ground on this war was shifting even as they recovered from the first true battle.

Nyssa drew back from her admiration and cooing over the baby. She gave Leksander a serious look. "I know it was your blade in Zephan's chest, but I cannot convince his father, the king, that it wasn't an angeling who put it there." She flicked a look to Tajael, who apparently had been haplessly caught in the situation. "The Winter Court is nothing if not stubborn in believing what they wish."

"So what does that mean?" Leksander asked.

"War," Nyssa said gravely. "Not between Summer and Winter, although I can't guarantee that won't be the fall-out. But the Winter Court has rallied around their prince. Zephan has yet to die, as far as I can discern. I think the king has induced some kind of stasis—a magical healing coma, if you will—but the Court seeks vengeance for their fallen, favored son. The fae and angels are ancient enemies, cousin. This is larger than the House of Smoke. You dragons always think everything is about you, but it's not. This is about the fae. This has *always* been about the fae."

Leksander nodded, and Erelah knew the Truth of that far more than her mate probably did, although he understood most of it. The treaty would keep the Winter Court from attacking humans outright, and the House of Smoke as well, but the demon plague remained, and now with war between fae and angels... much was still very uncertain. It was not beyond imagining that the End of Times could still be near. Although, as she gazed at her beautiful daughter and the bright shining of her soul, it was hard to imagine how such a thing of righteousness could usher in a dark age.

Nyssa tipped her head. "I'll see you soon, cousin." Then she twisted and disappeared in a flash of light.

A moment of silence ensued, then Leonidas spoke. "Is she planning to be a regular visitor now?" he asked, aghast.

"I sincerely hope not," King Lucian said with a frown.

Leksander's focus was entirely for little Aurora. "She can visit if she likes. I wouldn't be here if it weren't for her." And it was clear that her mate was intent on enjoying every moment of the new life the fae queen had granted him. As was right and wise. Patience had always been her mate's strongest Virtue, including all those long years where he kept his True Love for her hidden, waiting for her to be ready for him. She was in awe of the goodness of her mate, and it thrummed her True Love stronger each moment she was with him.

Markos stepped forward, now that his immortal enemy had left. "My Dominion will attend to the events that will unfold from Aurora's birth. You needn't worry for her safety, dragon prince."

Leksander looked up. "You'll leave an angeling contingent as a guard, as we discussed."

"Yes." Markos turned to Erelah. "But Tajael will not be among them," he told her. "I have a special assignment for him."

Erelah frowned and glanced at Tajael. His face was inscrutable. Obedient. He was a true angeling of the light, strongest in the Virtues of any angeling she'd known. "What kind of assignment?" she asked Tajael.

"Guardian," Tajael said, evenly. But it made Erelah's stomach clench.

Guardian. When angelkind was deep in a war already started.

Tajael tipped his head to Markos. "I live to serve." He would take this duty, and gladly, no matter the risks. But Erelah already knew that about him.

Then a smallish angelsong came from her tiny daughter, drawing Erelah's attention there. The baby was rousing from her nap, the golden sparkle of her protection spell still glittering on her skin. Her blue eyes were staring intently up at her father's face, then her tiny hands reached for him. The smile on Leksander's face was contagious—it ran entirely around the room and landed on Erelah's face.

Then the miraculous happened.

Aurora *lifted* from Leksander's arms. *She was flying on magic.* Erelah's heart seized, and she dashed a look to Markos, to see if he was making this happen, but his face held a blank surprise like everyone else. And when Erelah looked back...

Aurora's snow-white wings had unfurled.

Clad only in a diaper, her blonde wisp of hair and her white wings, Erelah's daughter flew up to her father's face and touched her tiny hands to his cheeks.

The amazement on his face was reflected in every face in the room.

Erelah gasped in a laugh, then covered her mouth with both hands to contain her joy.

Little Aurora hummed her soft angelsong, still mesmerized by her father's face.

Leksander turned his wide eyes to Erelah. "Well, this is going to be a problem."

Erelah laughed again, not even trying to hold it back now. "I told you... *she is angeling.*"

Leksander then tried to hold his infant daughter, his large hands gently wrapping around her small body, and the baby allowed it, snuggling in once again, wings furling to stow away. For all intents and purposes, Aurora appeared to once again be a normal child.

A normal, world-changing, child.

Erelah slipped close to them both, and she cared not that the entire assemblage of the House of Smoke, its princes and princesses, dragons and angelings, and even her faction leader looked on…

She kissed the man she loved and embraced the child they made.

The world may go to war, but there could be no Sin in this True Love.

WANT MORE DRAGONS?

Make sure you grab Leonidas's backstory in Of Bards and Witches!

<u>CLICK HERE</u> to get Leonidas's story!

Of Bards and Witches
London, The Year of Our Lord 1600
Leonidas is a dragon shifter, a century into his allotted five,

and he's entranced by Master Shakespeare's theatre and the comely and lusty women of London's bankside. But when he finds a witch in the practice of her art in clear view of the stage, he must act… for dragons are the keepers of the peace between the mortal and immortal realms. But never has duty been so sweetly sexy and delicious to the touch as a witch whose very skin sparks pleasure. He becomes lost in his bed, breaking his own cardinal rule—never seduce a woman for more than a night. As one pleasure-drenched night bleeds into the next, he runs afoul of a danger he ought already know… **never cross a witch.**

<u>CLICK HERE</u> to get Of Bards and Witches

The House of Smoke has found its Happy Ending! But all is not well in the Immortal Realms. A war brews between angel and fae, and Aurora's birth will indeed usher in a new day for angelkind. One where a Fall from Lust is even more dangerously possible, and the angels and angelings of the light will be tempted by the sweet promise of Love…

Tajael (Fallen Angels 1)

Grab Tajael (Fallen Angels 1) today!

Subscribe to Alisa's newsletter for new releases and giveaways: https://smarturl.it/AWSubscribeTempted

Paranormal Romance Series by Alisa Woods

https://alisawoodsauthor.com/

DOT COM WOLVES

The Big Bad Wolf… is her boss.

RIVERWISE PRIVATE SECURITY

Three hot brothers fighting to keep wolf shifters safe.

WILDING PACK WOLVES

The ex-Army bodyguard of a beautiful heiress has a secret.

FALLEN IMMORTALS

A hot Dragon Prince needs a mate, before he turns feral.

FALLEN ANGELS

He's Guardian of a beautiful scientist and oh so Tempted.

LEGAL MAGICK

An incubus FBI agent, a billionaire witch, and someone spiking street drugs with deadly magic.

BROKEN SOULS

She's stumbled into the lair of desperate dragon shifters… and she's just what the Lord of the Lair needs.

To be the first to hear about new releases…

Subscribe to Alisa's Newsletter

https://alisawoodsauthor.com/free-story/

About the Author

Alisa Woods lives in the Midwest with her husband and family, but her heart will always belong to the beaches and mountains where she grew up. She writes sexy paranormal romances about complicated men and the strong women who love them. Her books explore the struggles we all have, where we resist—and succumb to—our most tempting vices as well as our greatest desires. No matter the challenge, Alisa firmly believes that hearts can mend and love will triumph over all.

www.AlisaWoodsAuthor.com